YOUR SPOUSE, MY SPONSOR

A HOOD ROMANCE BY

PEBBLES STARR

www.jadedpublications.com

ARE YOU ON OUR EMAIL LIST?

Text BOOKS to 44144 to

be the first to hear about new releases, contests,

and giveaways!

This novel is a work of fiction. Any reference to real people, events, establishments, or locales is intended only to give the fiction a sense of reality and authenticity. Other names, characters, and incidents occurring in the work are either the product of the author's imagination or are used fictitiously, as are those fictionalized events and events that involve real persons. Any character that happens to share the name of a person who is any acquaintance of the author, past or present, is purely coincidental and is in no way intended to be an actual account involving that person.

LOOSELY
BASED ON
TRUE EVENTS

1

"See, this is why I fuck with this place. The water's nice and hot, and the service is consistent. Not like that bullshit you took us to over there on Piedmont a few weeks back," Monica laughed.

Monica and Femi dipped their toes inside the pedicure bowl simultaneously. Every two weeks they met for either fill-ins or pedicures while catching each other up on the latest drama. Last week, Femi wanted to try somewhere new, but the service stunk and Monica wouldn't let her friend live that shit down.

Now in their early thirties, both women had been friends since freshman year in high school. Monica, who was slightly chubby, was a beautiful woman with coffee brown skin and a cherubic face. She looked a lot like television personality, Shekinah, and always wore her hair in an asymmetrical bob. She made a decent wage working full-time as a local celebrity stylist.

Femi, born to West Indian parents, was dark brown with wide, bright eyes, full lips, and a curvy figure. At 5'9, she was taller than average, and most people often told her she resembled Keisha from the movie *Belly*.

"If you want chair massage, the remote next to you," the Vietnamese nail technician said in broken English.

"Thank you," Femi smiled. Relaxing in the seat, she hit the button, and allowed the chair to kneed away her stress and tension. No more than two minutes later, her phone rang. The call was from an unrecognizable number, so she hesitated on answering it.

"What's up?" Monica asked, noticing something was wrong.

Femi sighed and ran a hand through her natural, long hair. Her husband never wanted her to wear weave, because he thought she looked better without it. She loved her sew-ins but she would do just about anything to keep him happy.

"Another unknown calling me," Femi said. "You know what the fuck that means."

Monica snorted and shook her head in disgust. "I don't see how you put up with it, Femi. That nigga got all these hoes calling you like he ain't got a whole fucking wife at home. The shit pisses me off and he ain't even my man."

"I'm just not gonna answer it." Femi placed her phone down on the small table next to her chair. It stopped ringing for a short period, but started again after a few seconds.

When it was obvious that she wouldn't pick up, a series of text messages poured in.

"Bitch, you a good one. I would've divorced that dirty dick dog years ago—"

"Monica!" Femi lashed out. She was embarrassed that customers and employees were in earshot. She also didn't need to be reminded about the STDs.

"I'm sorry, but it's true. I don't see how the fuck you deal. Are you his main or his mistress, 'cuz I don't fucking get it—"

"And you won't," Femi cut in. "He's *my* husband, Monica. You wouldn't understand. When was the last time you had a man, '06?"

"2005 to be exact," Monica corrected her. "And that's why...'cuz niggas ain't shit. You give them one hundred and muthafuckas can't even give fifty percent."

Femi's cellphone continued to ring, only adding to her list of frustrations. Unable to ignore the constant calls, she finally answered in a snappy tone. "What?!"

A sultry but raspy female's voice filled the speaker. "Did you get my pictures?" Trina asked. The sarcasm in her tone made Femi want to reach through the phone and slap her.

"Which one is it this time?" Monica asked in the background. She'd grown equally used to the phone calls from multiple women.

Sucking her teeth, Femi pulled the phone away from her face and looked at the texts. Her blood boiled after seeing a plethora of photos with Trina and her husband looking real cozy. In every picture he was either sleeping or caught off guard completely. The bitch had to sneak a pic just to capture a photo of him. It was pathetic.

"You're interrupting my foot scrub, hoe," Femi stated. Her husband hadn't been home in two weeks. Due to business he traveled a lot, so there was never no telling what the nigga was up to. "What the fuck do you want?" she asked, cutting to the chase. Femi put Trina on speaker, so that her girl could hear how ridiculous she sounded.

"I thought the pictures were pretty self-explanatory," Trina laughed. She wanted Femi's husband. That much was obvious.

"Hand me the phone. I'll tell the hoe off," Monica said with her palm outstretched. "Either give it here, or hang up on that bih."

Trina heard Monica in the distance. Desperate to get a reaction before Femi hung up, she said, "Did you know he got me pregnant a few months back?"

Femi's entire face grew hot. It felt as if her heart had dropped to the pit of her stomach. The entire nail salon had heard the bomb she dropped. If Trina were anywhere within arm's reach, Femi would've strangled her. Jumping out of the chair with soaking wet feet, she ran outside so no one would hear her tirade. "What the fuck did you just say?!"

Her man had the young hoes going crazy. Upset about the empty promises made to them, they had nothing better to do than to call and torment Femi. It seemed like every other month she went through the same shit, but he never changed, and she never left.

"You heard me. I ain't stutter! Yo' nigga got me pregnant. Wasn't too hard since he be nutting in this pussy every week." Trina laughed wickedly. She could tell by Femi's silence that she'd gotten to her. "Looks like our kids gon' be siblings."

"Over my dead body," Femi told her.

"It's already done, boo. Don't feel so fucking good, does it? Knowing that nigga knocked me up after making you burn your tubes. You must feel pretty fucking stupid—"

Trina's sentence was cut short after Monica grabbed the phone and hung up. She'd run outside to make sure her girl was okay. She had never seen Femi snap like that. Usually, she didn't let hoes get her out of her hookup, but today Trina had pushed her buttons.

"Fuck that bitch," Monica said. "She's probably lying just to get a rise out of you. Don't give that silly hoe the satisfaction."

"You know my husband just as well as I do. I doubt that bitch is lying, M. And whether she is or ain't, he had no right telling these hoes our fucking business!" Femi was livid that he would do something like that. What the hell was he thinking? He knew how she felt about getting her tubes tied. She'd only done it because he made her. Now she was being told that he'd gotten some random bitch pregnant behind her back. Femi was so hurt that she couldn't hold back the tears. "I'm gonna kill that dirty mothafucka!"

2

Seventeen-year old Kirby Caldwell multi-tasked between carrying a tray of food and drinks to the table of fine ass men straight ahead. Judging from their swagger and poise, they didn't look like they were from Philly. Couldn't be. The European designer clothing, shiny jewelry, and expensive cologne screamed foreign. Kirby was drawn to them instantly like moths to a flame. The boys she saw on an every day basis were certainly not of their caliber.

These niggas are the real deal. Ever since they walked in, Kirby had been wracking her brain about what they did for a living. They were far from being the blue-collar type. They had trouble written all over, but for some reason she was still drawn to them.

Maybe they're staying upstairs in the Windsor suites, Kirby thought to herself. The customers at the pub she worked at were mainly guests who took advantage of the discount offered by the hotel.

As soon as Kirby reached their table, she pushed her thoughts to the back of her mind. All four men were in deep in conversation prior to her arrival but stopped the minute she approached them.

Kirby felt odd as each man sized her up. It made her nervous, because she knew they were trying to decide if they appreciated what they saw. She was thin with A-cup breasts, small hips, and an ass she thought was too big for her tiny frame. In her opinion Kirby thought she was just average. Nothing special, but nothing too bad to look at. One of her admirers, on the other hand, held an entirely different sentiment.

"Aye, you got a tough lil' body on you, ma. That thing pokin' too. How old is you, if you don't mind me askin'?" Aviance's eyes traveled the length of Kirby's petite body. He loved a skinny bitch with a fat ass. Someone he could easily manhandle while sticking the pipe to.

At only 20, he was the most flamboyant of the quartet. They were only politicking over dinner, and the nigga had on two diamond chains and a sparkling diamond grill. If it weren't for the fact that he kept a shooter 'round him, he would've been robbed countless times.

Aviance was damn near blinding everyone in the establishment, but he loved showing off. He also loved gorgeous women, and never bit his tongue when it came to expressing it. A smirk pulled at his full lips as he admired what he saw. Kirby was definitely his type. He was just about to go in for the kill when his boss cut in.

"Ease up, bruh. Swear yo' ass don't know how to act whenever you see a bad bitch. My bad, you gotta excuse my nephew."

After hearing the word 'bitch', Kirby did an automatic double take. She started to check his ass when suddenly she noticed how fine he was. She damn near spilled the drinks looking.

Smooth midnight black skin, pearl white teeth, chiseled jawline, and muscular build. *Gotdamn.* He looked like an African king—like the tribal warriors she read about in her black History books. He was beautiful.

Castle looked every bit of the boss he was in a black Givenchy tee and black high top Giuseppes. A black and gray Louis Vuitton belt secured his tan designer jeans. He had $120,000 on his wrist like money grew on trees.

I bet his ass got a flock of hoes at his beck and call though, Kirby presumed. Although she told herself that, she tampered with the thought of possibly being one of them. It must've been nice. She then laughed inside after realizing how out of her league he was. There he sat, draped in expensive clothes and jewelry while she waited on tables.

Kirby imagined him only dating Beyonces and Rihannas anyway. *I got as much chance ending up with him as I do hitting the lottery,* she told herself. *Keep dreaming.*

Nervously clearing her throat, Kirby placed the dishes in their respectable places and rushed off before she embarrassed herself. Her best friend, McKenzie was patiently awaiting her arrival behind the bar. She, too, was a waitress at the pub they worked at. The quaint mom and pop restaurant didn't get much business other than that of hotel guests, so they stood around talking shit all day until it was time to clock out.

"Girl, I'm so fucking jealous. I was praying I got their section," McKenzie joked. "Them jawns fine as shit, ain't they. And that dark-skinned one could get the mothafucking business. I'm just saying." She had a weakness for chocolate men.

Although Kirby and McKenzie were like sisters, they were as different as night and day. At 18, McKenzie was a tall, slender redbone with mint green eyes, freckles, and reddish brown hair that she inherited from her white daddy. He had walked out on her when she was just two-years old. This was after his wife found out about his sidepiece. McKenzie was a product of messiness. She was also very promiscuous.

Sometimes Kirby wondered if she was that way because of what her father did. Kirby reserved her judgment since they were girls despite her mother's constant warnings about the company she kept. She had never really cared for McKenzie.

"I'm not gonna lie, they low-key had me nervous. I wish you had gotten their section too. I dread having to go back over there," Kirby laughed.

"Damn, Kirbz, you gotta stop acting so scared of niggas. I swear, every time you get in the presence of a dude you retreat—"

"Bullshit," Kirby argued.

"Bitch, you practically ran from that section," McKenzie reminded her. "Besides, name the last time you even dealt with a nigga...and kindergarten don't count—"

"Don't come for me, sweetie. I told you I dry pumped in the girl's bathroom once and you won't let that shit go," Kirby laughed.

"Bitch, that was your best and *only* experience," her friend teased. "You need to get you some real dick, and quit acting so timid." McKenzie often teased her friend about her virgin status.

"Don't try to come down on me just 'cuz my track record don't match yours. When I'm ready I will."

Instead of entertaining Kirby's low blow, McKenzie pointed back to the fellas' table. "*Ooh*, look. One of 'em still checking you out," she giggled. "That mothafucka is too damn fine. What'd you do to that man, bish?" Kirby was almost scared to crane her neck. "Girl, quit playing. I haven't done anything." When she finally turned to look she noticed Castle staring directly at her. Kirby didn't know it yet, but he had already staked his claim on the young woman.

***

Since Kirby's shift ended three hours before McKenzie's she wound up catching the bus alone. Once she was let off at her stop, she walked the rest of the way. The routine had become as normal as breathing. South Philly wasn't exactly a safe haven, but she'd been living there all her life.

Kirby often dreamt about the day she was able to move out the hood and buy her first whip. She already knew what she wanted: a pearl white Mercedes Benz with shiny chrome rims. Instead of saving up for her dream car, Kirby had to pay utility and hospital bills. Three years ago her mom, Leah lost her left breast to cancer. It went in remission for a little while, but was now back and more aggressive than ever. Leah's heaping medical expenses left them bankrupt. The government assistance helped out some, but it wasn't nearly enough to support a dying woman and her teenage children.

Kirby's brother, Kaleb was a year older than her and stayed in and out of jail. He'd done everything from robbing to stealing in order to provide for his family—but the law eventually caught up with him.

It had been two years since the police kicked her door off the hinges to apprehend him. They dragged Kaleb off faster than they were able to read his Miranda rights. He was only seventeen at the time. They charged him for stealing and flipping cars, and he was left to rot in a human zoo.

In the beginning, Kaleb used to write his sister religiously, but over time his communication eventually slowed down. She figured he might've just wanted to serve his time in solitude. Though Kirby missed him, she wouldn't dare become a burden. She didn't know what he was going through alone in prison, but she didn't want to add more to his plate with her troubles. Kirby figured the least she could do was take care of mom and hold things down until he was released— whenever that was.

All of a sudden, the light blaring of a horn interrupted Kirby's thoughts. She noticed a shiny black Rolls Royce ease alongside her. The driver of the fancy vehicle made sure to match his pace with her walking.

"Aye, why you out here walkin' alone, mama. You need a ride or somethin'?"

Kirby recognized the voice before she did the driver. Seeing him again, and so unexpectedly, made her nervous. He made her palms sweat and her stomach flip-flop. *Damn.* What was it about him that made her get butterflies and fall apart whenever she was in his presence? What the hell was he doing in her hood anyway?

Kirby looked around to make sure he wasn't talking to someone else. It seemed almost impossible for him to show an interest in her. Someone who was flat-chested and average at best. She wondered if he was fucking with her for the hell of it. It would've been a crude thing to do if he was.

Just keep walking.

Kirby told herself one thing, but her curiosity outweighed her common sense.

"Aye, don't act like you don't see me." The hint of humor in his tone was enough to let her know he wasn't too serious. "I ain't from 'round here but I know it ain't safe for a young lady to be walkin' alone. C'mon. I ain't gon' bite." Castle brought his car to a slow stop, reached over and opened the passenger door.

He was in Philly for business purposes, but on that side of town to visit one of his freaks—a badass stripper he'd met at *Onyx*. He was on his way to her crib when he saw something more promising from the corner of his eye. Nothing intrigued him more than the prospect of new pussy, so he did what any self-righteous nigga would. He pulled up on her ass.

Ironically, before he left the restaurant with his boys, Castle passed his number to McKenzie to give to Kirby who was in the restroom at the time. What he didn't know was that McKenzie had jealously ripped it up and tossed it out. On the low, she was mad he hadn't hollered at her first. She'd been checking for him too; she peeped Castle the minute he walked in, but it was obvious whom he was more interested in. Naturally, McKenzie wasn't feeling that shit. In her world, no man would choose Kirby over her. McKenzie believed cute light-skinned girls reigned supreme.

Unfortunately, she had no control over fate and pure coincidence. Somehow Castle and Kirby still ended up bumping into each other.

Kirby cautiously peered inside his ride to verify he was by himself. *I probably shouldn't*, she told herself. She had never actually climbed in the car with a total stranger before. Since a young girl she knew better than to ever do something so stupid.

Kirby knew what she should've done. She should have continued walking...but her legs had a mind of their own as they slowly approached his flashy car.

"Is it...safe?" Kirby asked shyly. Castle made her unashamedly bashful, and he knew it was because he intimidated her. Men of his caliber didn't speak to chicks like her. Hell, they barely even gave them a second look. Castle found her nervous demeanor cute.

Chuckling at her innocent question, he asked, "How old are you, baby girl?"

"...Seventeen."

Castle refused to tell her that he had a daughter a year younger than her. "Aye, look. You in good hands, lil' mama. I promise."

Kirby slowly climbed inside, sealing her fate as soon as she closed the door. She figured there was no harm in allowing him to take her home. Besides, it wasn't like she didn't find him attractive.

"Why's it so fuckin' dark in this city? Like damn. Tax money won't cover the cost of some streetlights 'round dis mufucka? Gotta feel like you walkin' through the 'hood blind folded or some shit. You be walkin' every day at this time?"

"Yeah, but usually I'm with my girl McKenzie. We work together and she stays a block from me."

"Oh, nah. You too damn pretty to be on foot," he said, shaking his head. "If you was my bitch, I wouldn't have yo' ass walkin'."

Wale's new album played softly through his custom speakers. His interior smelled of Clive Christian cologne and top quality loud. Kirby didn't smoke, but she was familiar with the scent because Kaleb once sold it. That boy had damn near done everything under the sun just to put food in the fridge. He'd sacrificed his freedom to take care of her and their mom.

"What's yo' address?" Castle asked.

Kirby rattled off where she lived before fastening her seatbelt. She shouldn't have been so comfortable with him, but for some reason she felt like she could trust him.

After plugging her address in his GPS, he retrieved the L tucked behind his ear. He'd dropped several stacks to have a police monitor installed so that he could track how close a squad car was. Twelve loved to fuck with a nigga with some paper.

"You chief?" Castle asked, holding up the blunt.

"No," she murmured.

"You a good girl, huh?"

Kirby shrugged. "I guess so."

"Shit, they say good girls are just bad girls that never got caught..." Castle passed the blunt to Kirby again in hopes that she would hit it. He hated a square bitch.

Surprisingly, Kirby grabbed it and took a light pull. A flurry of hoarse coughs came soon after. She felt like she'd hacked up an organ. She had never smoked a day in her life. Wheezing and hacking, Kirby quickly passed the L back to Castle.

He took a couple tokes before lowering his window. "You good?"

"Yes," Kirby struggled to say.

"So what's ya name, Virgin Lungs?"

She laughed a little. "Kirby. And yours?"

"Castle Maurice Black III."

Kirby loved how regal his name sounded. It fit him so well. "Is that your real name?" she asked.

Castle laughed and it warmed her heart. She noticed that he now had a gold bottom grill in. The single piece of jewelry alone cost more than her home was worth. "Baby girl, I'm too old for aliases and nicknames, and shit."

"What's too old?" Kirby asked curiously.

"A whole lot older than you, youngin'."

"How old?" she pressed.

"Guess."

"*Hmm.*" Kirby rested an index finger on her right cheek's dimple. "I'mma say... Thirty maybe...."

Castle nodded his head appreciatively. Her irrepressible innocence and naivety captivated him. She was young enough to be molded and groomed. That was the main reason he loved young hoes. "Close," he said. "Thirty-six."

"Oh."

Castle didn't miss the flatness in her tone. "What'chu mean 'oh'?" he chuckled. "That too old for you?"

Kirby paused. Castle made her nervous. She barely knew anything about him, but she was sure she'd never met anyone like him. There was an enigmatic aura that surrounded him; he had a boss-like presence. She envisioned him as a man in charge, but she had no idea to what extent. She might've fled if she knew he was top dog of a multi-million dollar drug operation.

"I'm not sure. I never dated anyone in their thirties."

"Do you date at all," was Castle's next question.

"...Not really," Kirby answered, slightly embarrassed. She thought about lying but it was what it was. The boys at her school weren't really checking for her, and the few who did were never taken seriously. Either that, or they just weren't her type.

"So you mean to tell me yo' ass never had a boyfriend before?" he asked. "You ain't gotta lie to me, baby girl. One thing about me, I hate a fuckin' liar—"

"I'm not lying," she promised.

"You ever fucked before?"

Kirby's cheeks flushed in embarrassment. She wasn't expecting such a bold question. "No," she squeaked out.

"You ain't ever fucked before. You ain't ever had a boyfriend before. Why do I find that shit so hard to believe? How come you never had a boyfriend?"

Kirby shrugged. "I don't know. No one's really grabbed my interest, I guess."

"That's 'cuz you ain't ever fucked with a real nigga."

Castle slowly eased his car in front of Kirby's house. The building he pulled in front of hardly looked livable, but it was the destination his navigational system had led him to.

Kirby took her time unfastening her seatbelt. "Where you from, if you don't mind me asking. You mentioned you weren't from around here...and you have an accent."

"Oh yeah?" Castle chuckled, and his grill sparkled. "I'm from Atlanta, baby. Born and raised."

"That's cool. I hear a lot about Atlanta. What's it like?"

"Like Black Hollywood."

It sounded like somewhere she'd like to one-day visit. Lingering on the doorknob, Kirby almost didn't want to leave, but she knew her mother was waiting on her. As her health gradually degenerated, she had become increasingly immobile. Kirby couldn't leave her alone for extended periods.

"Shit, take my number though," he told her. "I'm only in town for a couple days, then I'm headed to Vegas. You ever been?"

"I never even left Philadelphia."

"Real shit? Damn. That's all bad. Fuck with me then. We could fly out together. It's fight weekend so shit's gon' be crazy."

"Fight weekend? What's that?"

Castle looked over at Kirby in disbelief. "You don't get out much, do you? Just a small city girl that ain't 'een stepped foot in the real world."

Kirby shrugged. She didn't have a comeback.

"Floyd and Pacquiao fightin' at the MGM."

"Who are they?"

Castle chuckled. "Boxers. Damn, baby. You live under a rock? You must not be into social media."

"Not really. Between work and school I barely have time to keep up with entertainment."

Castle loved that she wasn't big on social media. "I dig that. And ain't nothin' to be sorry about," he said. "You handlin' ya business. I like that shit. I can respect it. But yeah, like I was sayin', it's gon' be dope. I'm tryin' to brush shoulders with stars. You should fuck with a nigga. I'd show you a good time." He tried to gauge her interest with talk of celebrities.

"I can't just up and leave. I have to take care of my mama. She can't stay alone for long periods of time."

"Why? What's wrong with her?"

"She's...sick." Kirby wasn't ready to tell him that Leah was dying of cancer.

"Lemme handle that fuh you then," he offered.

"How?"

Castle shrugged like it was no big deal. "Shit, I'll pay somebody to do that."

Kirby laughed as if he'd said a joke. When she realized he was dead serious, she stopped and stared at him. She then thought about the crisp hundred-dollar tip he'd left her at the pub. "You really are for real, ain't you?"

"Do I look like a nigga that play games?" Castle took her hand in his, gently caressing her knuckles. His hands were large, rough and calloused in comparison to her smaller, softer ones. Years of prison, slinging, and gun toting had hardened him.

"No. But what about school?" Kirby asked. "I still have a couple weeks left 'til graduation—"

"Couple weeks?" he scoffed. "That's it? Well, shit, I guess we'll get up next time then. Gon' 'head and finish up ya'll lil' school year. There may be other opportunities."

Kirby didn't like the way that sounded. Castle made it seem as if she might not see him again after that day, and she wasn't feeling that.

"What if I *did* wanna go though," Kirby suddenly said. "We barely know each other...shouldn't we get to know each other first? I mean I never did this before..."

Castle could see that she was toying with the idea. Young and naïve, she couldn't help being gullible. Kirby was pure like raw cocaine—and just as lethal. Castle knew the consequences for fucking with an underage girl, but he still wanted her.

She had one of two choices. She could take the blue pill and return to her boring, everyday life while struggling to make ends meet. Or...she could take the red pill and allow Castle to make a woman out of her young ass.

"We can get to know each other on this lil' trip." Castle reached over and trailed his fingertip along her thigh. He had a solution for every excuse she hit him with. Kirby had actually run out of them altogether.

"I...I still don't know," she hesitated. "I...Maybe I need time to think about it."

"I'm leaving Thursday. So don't take too long to think about it, aight."

"I won't..." Kirby could feel things heating up between them. She'd never felt so much intensity with a guy before. "I'll call you," she said, opening the passenger door

"I'll be waitin'," he smiled. Castle enjoyed a good cat-and-mouse game, just as long as the other person made it worthwhile. He could smell that tight, illicitly sweet pussy from his seat. There was no pussy better than virgin pussy.

She bullshitting right now, but she'll be mine in no time, Castle told himself. He'd make sure of that.

Kirby carefully climbed out and headed towards her house. As she ascended the cracked stone steps, she could feel Castle's dark eyes penetrating her. If she could've saw into the future, she would've ran without looking back. She would've never climbed in his shiny Rolls Royce...and she certainly wouldn't have called him.

It was an inauspicious beginning to a long and complex relationship.

3

"Bitch, are you fucking serious? Why the hell did you tell him you had to think about it? You should've gone when he asked. No way I would've passed up on an opportunity like that," McKenzie said.

Since Kirby and Castle still somehow found their way to each other, she couldn't even hate. Hell, it was about time her friend got some action anyway. The bitch acted like she was scared of dick in McKenzie's opinion.

Kirby multi-tasked between flexi-rodding her hair and listening to her friend bitch about her not going to Vegas. She'd told Castle that she needed time, but she never even bothered to call. Truth was, he intimidated her.

Lying across Kirby's bed, McKenzie flipped through an outdated magazine. Whenever her mother had company, she fled to Kirby's house. Kirby thought it was just because McKenzie didn't like her mother's boyfriends, but the truth was one had raped her when she was 15. Ever since, she tried to avoid them at all costs.

"I ain't gonna hear the end of this shit, am I?" Kirby asked. "Anyway, he was damn near twice my age—"

"If he ain't care why you tripping?" McKenzie asked.

Something told her Castle may have been trouble, but Kirby was still curious about him. She wondered if his lips were soft, and if his skin was as smooth as it looked. She wanted to see him again, and yet she couldn't even bring herself to hit him up.

McKenzie shrugged. "I just think you made a dumb move. That's all. He was trying to fly you out to kick it. Any bitch would've jumped on that shit no questions asked." Closing the magazine, she tossed it on the bed, and stood up. "Jesus, Kirby. You are so fucking skinny. Your lil' ass need to start eating more."

"Shut up!" Kirby was already sensitive about her tiny figure. She hated her high metabolism.

"I'm serious."

"Can we get off my body already? And it don't even matter now. It's too late," Kirby said. "It's already Thursday. He's probably touched down and everything. He ain't thinking about my ass. Besides, I couldn't just leave my mama. She would flip."

"Girl! I could've watched yo' stankin' ass mama while you did your thing."

Kirby cut her eyes at McKenzie. "Bitch, don't call my mama stankin'," she said.

Since McKenzie couldn't fight to save her life, she quickly said, "Chill, I'm just playing. But that would've been perfect though. It wouldn't have been a problem finding someone to cover your shifts at work. I'd be here with Leah so you wouldn't have had shit to worry about. You know it ain't like my bitch ass mama'll let me fuck in my crib. At least at your place, I'd be free to do whatever I wanted. And the fact that I'm taking care of your mom would've been the perfect excuse. It was foolproof, Kirby! *Ugh*! Why do you always have to ruin everything for me?"

Kirby laughed. "Um...Selfish much? I thought this was about me and Castle."

"I'm just saying though. Anyway, you talked to your brother lately?"

Kirby's playful mood quickly vanished. Her brother was a sensitive subject. "No," she mumbled. "And I'm changing the topic now. Back to Castle, he offered to hire someone to look after my mom. But I don't know how she would feel about that. You know how funny acting she is. I mean, don't get me wrong. I want to go. I really want to...but..."

"But what, Kirby?" McKenzie pressed. "Right now, it just sounds like you making a bunch of bullshit excuses. School's almost over anyway. We 'bouta graduate. Fuck the few days you'll miss. I say you should've gone for it. YOLO."

Kirby chewed on her bottom lip as she thought about what her friend was saying. It was a habit she often did whenever she was in deep thought.

"You really think I should've gone, huh...?"

"Like I said...you only live once..."

***

The following afternoon, Castle's nephew Grip decided to let loose some energy in the local boxing gym. He used to play football during his earlier high school days, but fell into the street life around 16. He dropped out in his senior year after realizing the shit wasn't for him. Now at 20, he served as an enforcer for his uncle's drug operation.

Grip was 6"3 with a muscular build and dreads that reached a little past his shoulders. Thick long lashes covered his dark almond-shaped eyes, and light stubble surrounded his full lips. An array of decorative artwork covered his rich caramel skin. The ones that stood out the most were the portrait of his parents and the skull and roses tattooed on the back of his hands.

Because of his size, motherfuckers knew better than to try him. That was why Castle took him under his wing after his father died.

Grip's dad, Benedict was the man since the day he crawled out of his mama's twat. Born with a natural hustler's instinct, he'd had his hand in every type of illegal business there was; but it was the drug game that ultimately fed him. At the tender age of 21, Benny established one of the largest and most profitable organizations in the South. Authorities dubbed him and his empire the Royal Black Mafia because of their monarchical names.

Benny and his crew effortlessly took over the dope game in the mid 90s. Using his gift of gab, he was able to build allies with plugs and law enforcement alike. Everyone loved him. He was a big guy with an even bigger personality, a people magnet.

Castle, on the other hand, felt a different way. Since childhood, he'd always lived in his older brother's shadow. It seemed like everyone favored Benny over him, and he hated the shit.

Instead of bitching about it, Castle patiently waited for his moment to triumph. After Benny was killed, his position was handed down to his younger brother. There were more fitting men who should've taken over, but Castle was kin and next in line. He ran the empire with an iron fist, eliminating competition and doubling profits in two short years.

Grip would've lost respect for his uncle if he knew about all the underhanded shit he did while his father was still alive. Castle had stolen from Benny, pursued unlawful ventures behind his back, and even fucked his baby mama once.

Benny never suspected that the only snake in his camp was his own brother. He damn sure wasn't prepared when Castle emptied a clip in him and staged it to look like a robbery. That was one secret Castle planned on taking to his grave.

Jealousy was a destructive emotion.

Grip would've lost it if he knew he was protecting the same man who'd murdered his father. He took two massive swings at the heavy bag, nearly knocking them off the hook.

Irony could be a bitch.

Grip had his dad's massive height, and his Grenadian mother's looks. His mom, Naomi was originally from the islands but had relocated to Philadelphia in her early twenties. One of Benny's connects lived there, so he was visiting because of business. She was standing on her mama's porch when he drove by and saw her. She was so damn cute, he had to stop and say something. Suave and charismatic by nature, it didn't take long for Benny to sweep her off her feet.

Benedict was everything she wanted in a man and more, and he spoiled her endlessly. Over time she got greedy though and allowed the money to change her. Then she took an ultimate low when she had a one-night stand with Castle. Guilt eventually caused depression, and she fell back into attending church. Wanting to start her life over, Naomi decided it was best to part ways with Benny and his dangerous lifestyle. She was six months pregnant at the time of her decision. She chose to raise Grip away from his unlawful business, so she stayed in Philly and Benny in ATL. Because Naomi was saved she refused to take his drug money. Instead of letting Benny spoil her like he used to, she chose to raise Grip alone in hopes that he'd learn the meaning of hard work and morals. She did the best she could until she was involved in a fatal car accident. Grip was 17 at the time. Benny stepped up to the plate once he was granted full custody. Moving Grip down to Georgia, he tried to do right by him.

Grip's training session was interrupted after his phone rang. Wiping the sweat off his brow, he walked over to his iPhone lying on the nearby bench. "Yo'."

"Where you at, boy? I know yo' ass still ain't dickin' around in the A. I need you in Vegas pronto," Castle told him. "Got some shit I need you to handle."

"Damn, right now? I'm at the gym," Grip said with an attitude.

"Nah, mufucka, next year. Yeah, nigga, right now," Castle snapped. "So look, in 'bout two hours I gotta jet comin' to pick you up. I don't wanna say too much on the line...I'mma hit you with a text with all the info."

"Fa'sho."

"I'll get up with you later. Don't disappoint me."

"I never do, unc'."

After disconnecting, a series of incoming text messages came in. Grip's uncle wanted him to oversee the transportation of his product to Nevada. They had talked about the trip earlier in the week, but honestly he had forgot all about it.

Grip wasn't too thrilled about the trip to Vegas. Honestly, he could take it or leave it. The only reason he was going in the first place was because Castle needed him to.

Grip didn't know it at the time, but a huge surprise awaited him in Sin City.

4

Kirby had to pinch herself after she landed at *McCarran International Airport.* After calling Castle the night she spoke with McKenzie, he flew her out first class the very next morning.

Kirby looked like a lost, little puppy as she navigated through the airport towards ground transportation. An assortment of colorful slot machines littered the floors. She couldn't believe she was actually there.

Once Kirby finally stepped out of the crowded airport, she took in her surroundings. She had never laid eyes on an actual palm tree in all her life. The air even smelled different. Las Vegas was beautiful.

Kirby flagged down the next yellow cab in cue. Castle had wired her $1000 just so she could have something in her pocket during the solo trip there.

The Ethiopian driver eagerly pulled up to the curb, hopped out and helped Kirby with her luggage. Every so often he stole a glance at her cleavage. Kirby's small breasts peaked through the white V-neck she was wearing with no bra underneath.

"My apologies, ma'am. You are so beautiful."

The crazy thing was, he hadn't even made eye contact once.

Kirby tried to pretend she wasn't creeped out by the fifty-something year old man. Climbing inside, she settled in and sent a text to Castle letting him know she'd landed and was on her way to the *MGM*.

Kirby was excited to tour a city that wasn't her hometown. She'd never left Philadelphia before, and it was refreshing to be somewhere new. She was also nervous about seeing Castle again. He made her uneasy, vulnerable, and excited all in the same breath.

Kirby took in the colorful lights, high-rises, and scenery on the way to the hotel. The *MGM* was even more impressive than she imagined.

After being dropped off, Kirby made her way to the front desk where she checked in and was provided a key card. Castle had added her name to his room upon her arrival.

Kirby attempted to call him on the way up, but he didn't answer. When she finally reached his room, she politely knocked first but no one came. Kirby then went ahead and let herself in—her mouth practically hit the floor when she saw how massive his corner suite was. He had one of the finest rooms the hotel offered. Castle didn't believe in half-assing shit he did. Whenever he did something, he went all out.

"Castle?" Kirby called out.

She heard shower water running in the distance. She thought about knocking on the bathroom door, but didn't want to interrupt him. *What if I see some shit I'm not ready to see*, she asked herself. The only dicks Kirby had ever seen were the ones in porn.

Setting her luggage in the corner of the suite, Kirby walked over to the large windows and looked out. She could see the entire strip from where she stood. The city was lively, and unlike anything she'd ever witnessed.

The sudden sound of movement caused her to turn around. Kirby's breath instantly caught in her chest when she saw Castle standing there in nothing but a towel wrapped around his waist. He was bow-legged, so his stance was everything.

Tiny beads of water glistened on his smooth, black sin. Castle's body was ripped to perfection, his abs and pecks bulging, as if beckoning her to touch them. He looked like an African God.

How could a man be so beautiful?

Kirby tried not to stare at the elephant imprint of his dick behind the towel. Even while flaccid, she could clearly see that homeboy was packing. She also noticed several scars on his torso from when he'd been shot back in 2000.

"I ain't even hear you come in." A smile tugged at the corners of his lips. The effect he had on Kirby was dangerous.

"I called and texted," she said. Nervously clearing her throat, she looked around the suite a second time. It felt odd every time they made eye contact. "This is beautiful, Castle. I'm not used to fancy stuff like this."

"You gon' be my bitch, so you betta get used to it."

Kirby loved the way that sounded.

Castle slowly walked over to her and placed a soft kiss on her forehead. "How was the flight, bay?"

The close contact made her nipples harden. "It was...uh..." Kirby nervously cleared her throat. He always made her tense up whenever they were in close proximity. "It was straight. For it to be my first time on a plane, I thought I did good."

"You hungry?"

"Starving. I only had a bag of chips on the plane."

"Sounds like daddy needs to feed you then. Lemme get dressed real quick, and we'll grab somethin' to eat."

"Okay. Bet."

Castle held Kirby's hand everywhere they went. It made her feel worthy and special, like they were actually an item even though they technically weren't official. For lunch, Castle treated her to sushi at the 5-star *Bar Masa*. It was Kirby's first time ever trying it, and she was surprised to find she enjoyed the eel ngiri. She loved how Castle was able to introduce her to new things.

After getting their fill on seafood, they rode around the city together in his topless Bentley Coupe. Kirby felt like she was in a dream as the wind blew through her hair. After taking her on a brief tour of the city, Castle returned to the *MGM* where he entertained himself with a few games of roulette.

"I'm confused," Kirby spoke up. "I don't know how any of this works. Will you explain it to me."

"Of course," he said. "I'mma teach you everything, bay." There was double meaning behind his statement. He'd have Kirby counting his money, and sucking and fucking like a pro in no time.

In just a couple short hours, Castle racked up eight bands. Collecting his earnings, he and Kirby went to the bets section where he put 7 grand on Floyd, and gave Kirby the last thousand to put on him as well. She couldn't help but wonder what he did for a living. Although she wanted to ask, she didn't quite want to overstep her boundaries.

Maybe he'll tell me when he's ready, she figured.

It was nearing sunset when Castle told her he had to handle some business with his boys. "Look, I'm 'bout to slide for a couple hours. Find somethin' to do to up here to keep you entertained. Then when I get back, we'll get dressed and hit a club or some shit."

"I could just waste time downstairs at the casino—"

Castle quickly cut her off. "Nah, I don't want you walkin' 'round down there. I don't need them thirsty ass niggas comin' at you. I'll have to break a nigga's jaw. Stay up here and wait for me, bay. I promise I won't be long."

"Okay. I'll stay up here," Kirby agreed.

"I wanna show you off tonight. Wear red. That's my favorite color."

Kirby smiled and blushed. She had the perfect dress. She'd borrowed it from McKenzie who "borrowed" it from her mom after receiving the gift from one of her boyfriends. The $800 Herve Ledger dress had been passed through more hands than a baton.

44

"Okay," she mumbled. Castle had her wrapped around his finger.

Sitting on the edge of his massive king size bed, she watched him pull on a fresh pair of Yeezy's.

After grabbing his python wallet, Castle walked over to her and knelt down so that they were eye level. "Gimme a kiss 'fore I go."

Kirby hesitated for a second. She was caught off guard by his demand.

Castle chuckled at her innocence. He figured she had never kissed a nigga before, but he was wrong. "Am I intimidating? Why you so bashful? Come here."

Ever so gently, he cupped Kirby's chin and pressed his lips against hers. A true Leo, he was aggressively passionate. Slowly, snaking his tongue inside her mouth, Castle kissed and sucked the taste of peppermint right off her tongue. A low moan escaped Kirby's throat. His lips were softer than she'd imagined.

She practically lost it when he began sucking on her bottom lip. His hand left her chin and gently clasped her throat. He wanted to turn her young ass out right then and there, but he knew she wasn't ready for the D. First, he had to break her in. Fuck her mind, and the pussy will come on its own. That was his motto.

"*Mmm*. Lemme stop. You ain't ready, lil' lady." Castle forced himself to pull away. She had him harder than a Calculus test.

Kirby was still breathless; she didn't want it to end. She'd remember their first kiss forever.

"I'll be back in a minute, aight."

"Okay. See you soon."

Castle was pleased with the neediness he saw in her eyes. She didn't want a nigga to leave, but he had business he had to tend to.

After the door closed behind him, Kirby excitedly hopped up and FaceTimed McKenzie. She'd gotten the iPhone 4S from a guy in the hood that sold them for the low.

"Bitch, you there?" McKenzie answered immediately.

"Yes! Yes! Look!" Kirby flipped the camera so that she could see Castle's impressive suite. She then walked over to the window so that McKenzie could take in the beautiful skyline.

"I bet ya ass glad that you took my advice now, right? Have ya'll fucked yet? Do he gotta big dick?"

"Damn, bitch. My plane only landed a few hours ago. Relax," Kirby laughed. "But yeah, it's amazing out here. And Castle is super sweet. He holds my hand and opens the doors wherever we go like the perfect gentleman. He even compliments me. It's like we're already a couple." Kirby was gone. All she knew was that she liked him, and he liked her.

"Whoa there, Kemosabe. Play it cool," McKenzie told her. "Remember, niggas hate a thirsty bitch. Act unfazed and for God's sake don't act like a damn rookie." McKenzie was so concerned about how her friend would be perceived, when she should've been more worried about her well-being.

Kirby was in a different state with a man she barely knew.

"I'mma just act like myself. It seems to be working for me, so far. Anyway, how's my mother?"

"She cool," McKenzie said nonchalantly.

Truth be told, she hadn't checked on her in hours. She was too concerned with who was coming over that night. If Kirby's brother Kaleb were out, she would've given anything for it to be him. They never fucked, but she sucked his dick on a few occasions even when he had a girl at the time. McKenzie—along with every other girl in her hood—had always secretly been in love with Kaleb. Kirby didn't know it, but McKenzie wrote to him every now and then, though he rarely responded. And when he did it was only to ask for provocative photos and money on his Green Dot.

"Thanks, McKenzie," Kirby said. "For everything."

"You got it, boo. No problem. Anyway, guess who's stopping over tonight to keep me company?"

"Who?" Kirby asked. She wasn't too crazy about McKenzie having boys in her house, but she knew the stipulations when she agreed to let her stay.

"Marcus Sears."

There was a brief pause on Kirby's end. "Marcus Sears from our chemistry class? That Marcus?"

McKenzie giggled innocently. "Yeah."

Kirby released a deep sigh before pinching the bridge of her nose. "Bitch, don't play. You know that's the one I have a crush on—"

"Well, hell. You never made a move. Plus, I figured you were with ole' boy now and you wouldn't care," she said in her defense. "And I heard Marcus talking to his boys one time, and he said he don't even like dark brown girls. You would've been wasting your time anyway," McKenzie fibbed. She'd been a habitual liar since the day she could speak. "You know what though? Never mind. I'll spare Marcus and let you have him."

Let me have him? Kirby didn't like the sound of that shit at all. For years McKenzie had been doing the same thing. She just had to have whatever boy Kirby was momentarily interested in. If Kirby didn't know any better she'd think McKenzie got a kick out of doing the shit on purpose.

Kirby thought about telling her about herself, but then Castle came to mind. Marcus was a joke in comparison. *Why am I even trippin'? She can have that dusty ass nigga. I gotta real one right here.*

"No, it's cool. Go for it," Kirby told her. "You right. I don't care."

"You sure?" McKenzie asked.

"You got it. You can have him," Kirby reassured her.

"Thanks, sis. I appreciate you being so cool about it."

Whatever bitch, Kirby thought.

"Promise we won't fuck in ya bed. Enjoy yourself, okay. And don't do anything I wouldn't do."

"I'll try my best."

***

Castle and his small entourage arrived at the private landing strip a little after 9 p.m. In attendance were his boys Aviance, Anderson, and his accountant, Boomer. A pudgy, brown-skinned guy with a short box fade, Boomer landed the job simply because he was once a mathematics major.

Aviance balanced his roles as dealer and muscle, but he stayed with Castle so much one would've assumed he was his protégée. Castle had taken them all under his wing when they were nothing more than teenage delinquents. When society turned their backs on them, he came and blessed them with a position in his business.

Together, all four men approached the cocaine-laden commercial jet, carrying six million worth of pure. Shortly after, the door opened and Grip and the pilot descended the stairs. After exchanging dap Castle asked, "How was the flight, kid?"

"No troubles. Smooth sailing."

The trip went just as Castle predicted. A few months back, they did a dry run without any narcotics to see if authorities would hinder them.

"Cool. Cool. Let's get this mufucka unloaded then." Castle boarded the jet and immediately went to stripping away the panels. In order to avoid detection, they'd crammed bricks in every nook and cranny, including underneath the seats and floorboards. Once he realized something wasn't right, Castle turned around and glared at the pilot. "Mufucka, this don't look like seven hundred pounds."

Adrian, the pilot, immediately started sweating bullets. He, along with everyone else, knew how horrible Castle's temper was.

"I—I thought you said a q—quarter shy of five-hundred—"

"Stop stutterin', dummy and tell me where my shit is 'fore I put a hole in ya chest."

Grip stepped up in an attempt to defend the pilot. He was forever trying to save someone's ass from becoming a victim to his uncle's rage. "Unc', chill—"

Castle had no chill though as he snatched out his gun.

"I ain't calmin' the fuck down 'til I get the rest of my shit, Adrian! If you wanna make it home to dem nappy headed lil' girls of yours, I suggest you start talkin'!"

Adrian backed up in fear. He never anticipated that today would be his last. He knew better than to get involved with the mafia, but ten racks to transport was too tempting to pass up. The money, however, wasn't worth his life.

"C—Castle, I swear...I—I thought—"

"You thought what?" he cut in. "You thought I wouldn't pop ya ass off one fuck up? Nigga, where my shit at? I know ya ass ain't cop a few keys for yaself—"

"Castle, on my soul, I didn't! I thought you said—"

Adrian's voice trailed off after Castle cocked the gun and aimed at his chest. They were all on the commercial jet and out of view. With a silencer screwed on the end of his gun, he could lay him down with no witnesses.

"Grip, pass me dat pillow, fam," Castle instructed. His nephew had used it to get comfortable on the flight, but now it would come in handy for muffling the sound of gunshots.

Grip snatched the pillow and handed it to Castle. "I didn't come down here for this bullshit," he mumbled.

Adrian immediately saw his life flash before his eyes. "Castle, don't do this man. I got two lil' daughters—"

"I'on give a fuck about them lil' hoes!"

"It was an honest mistake—a miscommunication," Adrian cried.

Castle approached Adrian with his heat, and the terrified man instantly dropped to his knees. Castle started laughing when he began praying to God for mercy.

"Man, get'cho dumb ass up. I was only fuckin' with you. Chill out."

Everyone on board released the breaths they were holding in. Castle had built up so much intensity that they all expected Adrian to be murdered.

Grip shook his head at his uncle's antics. "You gotta real fucked up sense of humor, man." He didn't see a damn thing funny. Castle was a crude, cynical mothafucka. He didn't even care that he'd almost made Adrian piss himself.

"This is all of it," Castle told them. "Ya'll niggas can start unloading. I'mma head back to the hotel and change. I'll get up with ya'll later on. I got my new lil' Philly dip waitin' on me."

5

Grip thought his eyes were playing tricks on him when he saw who Castle's new lil' Philly dip was. It was a quarter after 11, and he and his new love interest had just walked in *Draís* together. It wasn't the fact that she looked much younger than Castle that left Grip awestruck. It was actually because he knew her personally...

You gotta be kiddin' me, Grip thought. *For real though?*

Kirby didn't notice him immediately as she stood shyly beside Castle, looking out of place. Grip, and a few of the niggas were posted in VIP when the captain of their crew arrived fashionably late. Now that business was taken care of, they were blowing cash and sipping codeine like it was Kool-Aid. A colorful selection of women was sprinkled throughout their section, each one hoping to claim a made man. Same shit. Different state.

Aviance, draped in every piece of jewelry he owned was busy making Instagram videos to show off his wealth. Castle always told him 'less shining and more grinding', but he insisted on being flashy.

Grip would've never expected to see Kirby in Las Vegas...He was staring so hard that he'd almost forgotten a bitch was sitting right in his lap.

When her eyes finally landed on Grip's, they lingered for a bit. Apparently, she too, was surprised by the presence of an old friend. They used to attend the same high school...and once they'd even shared an intimate encounter...

"Wassup, Tic Tac?"

Startled by the hand that pinched her ass, Kirby practically dropped her textbooks. There was only one person who called her by that name because of her small breasts. Gavin Carmichael never missed an opportunity to tease her. It was like he enjoyed fucking with her. Then again, she was the only girl he gave the most attention and energy to. One time, Kirby thought he might've even liked her, but she quickly talked herself out of believing it.

Boys weren't falling over themselves to be with her. They were too busy chasing after girls like McKenzie.

No one was checking for her...or so she thought.

"I wish you would stop calling me that," Kirby said with her back to him. She didn't want him to see that she was in fact blushing. Grip made her nervous. He earned the title of "bad boy" after a few on-site arrests. After dropping out of the football team in 10th grade,

Grip started selling bud to the students and staff. He was following in his father's footsteps and he didn't even know it.

"What'chu want me to call you then?" Grip asked. "My girl?"

Kirby quickly turned him down. "Eww, no!"

"Don't eww me, buster. Eww yaself, skinny ass. Lookin' like a lil' boy from the back."

"If you don't like it why you talking to me?" Kirby countered.

"Maybe 'cuz I like you..."

"Well, I don't like you. And I'm not your girl." Kirby closed her locker and turned to look at him.

Grip wasn't used to girls blowing him off. She was going to hear him out one way or another. "Quit trippin', Kirby. You know I was just fuckin' with you," he said. "Lighten up. You always actin' like you got this barrier up when I come around. You like that with all the niggas or just me?"

"I'm not trying to get sucked in your game, Gavin."

He looked offended. "What game is that?"

"You expect me to believe that you're interested in me?"

"Why can't I be?"

"Did McKenzie try to hook you up with me?"

"Look, I don't know who the fuck McKenzie is or why you askin' me all these questions," he said. "I just dig that you low key. You not like these other girls. And you cute as shit."

"Oh, so now I'm cute? You were just telling me I look like a little boy. What does that make you?" she teased.

Gavin laughed. "Man, chill out, buster. I told you I was fuckin' with you." He scooted closer. "Let's tongue kiss and make up."

"Um...No."

"Why? You can't kiss or somethin'?" he asked. "I bet'cho square never even kissed before. Have you?"

Kirby caught herself right before she could say no. "Of course I have. Who hasn't kissed?"

Grip surprised her when he stole one for himself. The second time he grabbed her ass she didn't jump. He'd caught her off guard, but she would be lying if she said she didn't like his mannishness.

After Grip pulled back, she stood there surprised, hoping and praying he did it again. She was glad when she got her wish. During the second kiss their tongues mated. Kirby had no idea how amateurish she looked. Truthfully, she didn't know what the hell she was doing.

After pulling apart, Grip wiped his wet mouth and laughed. "Yo' ass was flexin'. You ain't never kissed before. That sloppy ass shit. I bet you never fucked before either, huh?"

"Grip—"

"You be fuckin' these niggas?" he demanded to know.

"Does it matter?"

"Fuck you think? I told you I'm feelin' you. You think I'mma be straight with you fuckin' these niggas? Only nigga should be pokin' dat mufucka is me."

"You talking to me like I'm already your girl."

"Might just be..."

"Since when?"

Grip tugged on Kirby's shirt, pulling her closer to him. "Don't fuck with me. You know what's up," he said, gazing down in her eyes. He was a giant to her 5"3 stature. "I'mma be the nigga to break you in. Just watch."

Kirby tried not to look intimidated. Grip made her nervous since secretly she liked him too. "Whatever. Anyway, what was that for?" she asked in regards to the kiss.

Grip didn't let go of her shirt. It was almost like he wanted every nigga passing by to know she was his. "I just wanted to know if you could kiss or not," he said. "Don't worry though. We got time for practice..." Grip squeezed her ass a third time. "We got time for a lot of shit." He was about to kiss her again until he looked up and saw the principal and his social worker approaching them. "Shit." He knew it was trouble. That was the only reason those two motherfuckers were ever together. Grip was surprised he didn't see his P.O. following closely behind.

"Damn. Aye look, I need you to hold this for me." Grip quickly passed her the zip in his backpack before anyone could see. "Put it in yo' locker."

"Grip—"

"Just do it."

Kirby unwillingly took the drugs and shoved them in her locker. Grip owed her big time for that shit.

"Gavin, I need you to come with us," Principal Shane said once he reached them.

"Is everything cool?"

"Just come with us, please? I think it's best we speak in private."

Grip looked over at Kirby. "Look, I'm finna go. But I'mma meet you at ya locker after last bell. I wanna walk you home, aight."

Kirby figured that was when he would reclaim his drugs. She waited for him for over an hour after school ended, but he never showed. Sadly, his mother was killed that day. Benny came and whisked him away to Georgia, and she and Grip never saw each other again.

That was two years ago. Nothing could've prepared them for bumping into one another that night. Kirby tried her best to ignore the fact that Grip looked better with some age and muscle on him. He had dreads now, which were tied up under an Atlanta Braves fitted cap.

Kirby wasn't the only one appreciative of what she saw. Grip hadn't taken his eyes off her since she walked up. He stared at her body a bit too long, and Castle noticed it as well. Though he shouldn't have been, Grip found himself even more attracted to her than he was back then.

From what Grip could remember, Kirby never gave any dudes the time of day. She kept her head in the books and seemed low-key. That was what he liked most about her. Back then, he just knew she was a virgin, and he had dreams of one day breaking her in. He figured the opportunity had long since passed.

What the fuck is she doing here though, he wondered?

He would've never pegged Castle as her type. Evidently, she had a thing for old heads. *Maybe that explains why she ain't never wanna fuck with the niggas in school*, he figured.

Grip swallowed a bitter taste of resentment. It was some fucked up shit to see his uncle snag her in the end. If it wasn't for him relocating to Georgia, she might've been his.

Damn...It's finna be a long night, he told himself. Now that Grip knew Kirby was Castle's, he had no choice but to restrain his lust. The last thing he needed was to get caught up...but he'd be damned if Kirby didn't make it hard on a nigga.

***

Kirby was having a good ole' time until Castle showed his true colors later on that night. *Draís* was packed with K Camp performing, and everyone seemed to be having fun except her.

The entire day Castle showered Kirby with attention, so much so that she'd become spoiled. Feeding her game, he had easily made her feel she was the only one he had interest in. He'd placed her on a pedestal by introducing her as his girl to his boys, and it immediately went to her head. Castle had her confidence level on a thousand, but she quickly turned insecure when she saw all the beautiful women at his neck. It was no secret that Castle loved pussy, probably more than he did making cold, hard cash. Kirby was the only one not privy to the facts.

From the sideline, she watched with her arms folded as Castle entertained his flock of groupies. They peeped the fancy clothes, shiny jewelry, authoritative swag, and immediately saw dollar signs. Castle didn't mind; he loved the attention either way. Growing up, Benny was always the one who bagged all the bitches. Now that he was dead, and the attention was centered on Castle, he ate that shit up like it was his last meal.

While Kirby stared daggers at the man who should've been getting more acquainted with her, Grip was studying her from afar. Kirby looked beautiful that night in the form-fitting red dress she'd promised to wear for Castle. Sadly, the nigga didn't even see her. They'd come together, but from the looks of things he'd be leaving with someone else. Poor Kirby didn't know what she'd stepped into by getting involved with a nigga like him. Castle was insatiable. No one woman would ever be enough to fully satisfy him.

If Kirby had known that beforehand, she would've never agreed to fly out to Las

Vegas. She felt silly as she stood off to the side with jealousy coursing through her veins. She didn't feel pretty or worthy anymore. In silence, she watched him talk and laugh with the hoes like she wasn't present. She even peeped him squeeze the fake ass on one of them. Castle was fucked up off lean and Molly, and feeling himself as usual.

Since his uncle was preoccupied, Grip made his way over to Kirby to initiate small talk. "You don't look like you having fun," he said.

Kirby tore her icy stare away from Castle long enough to look up at Grip. "What do you think?" she asked sarcastically.

Grip shrugged. He thought about telling her to get used to it, but hating wasn't his steelo. Besides, she'd gotten her first taste of the real Castle Black.

"I wasn't expecting to see you here. How do you know him anyway?" Kirby asked.

"Castle's my uncle," Grip said flatly. "How do *you* know him?" He tried his best not to sound jealous as he asked the question. He was definitely feeling a way about seeing her there with him.

"It ain't important," she said. Kirby had an attitude because of how Castle was treating her, and she was taking it out on Grip like it was his fault.

"Fuck it then. I don't 'een wanna know."

After seeing that she'd offended him, Kirby quickly tried to clean up her act. "I met him at—"

"Nah, don't try to tell me now. I told you I ain't wanna know." After reversing the game, Grip walked away from her stuck up ass so she could vent in solitude.

Kirby went back to glaring at Castle from where she stood. He was now whispering in one of the girl's ear. *Damn. Can this nigga be any more inconsiderate*, she asked herself. Kirby thought about leaving and catching the cab back to his hotel, but she didn't want to give him the satisfaction of knowing how upset he'd made her. All of a sudden, McKenzie's words played over in her mind. *"Act unfazed."*

Kirby smiled devilishly. An idea suddenly came to mind. She knew exactly what to do now. *If he wants to play, then I will beat him at his own game.*

With her intentions set, Kirby walked over and grabbed the hand of a cute brown-skinned guy that'd been checking her out all night. He wasn't all that attractive but he would do. Gently pulling him towards her, she turned around and proceeded to dance seductively. From the way she grinded and pushed it back on him, one would've thought she'd been fucking for years. Every so often, she looked over in Castle's direction to see if he was looking. She was determined to give him a taste of his own medicine.

"I been checkin' on you since you walked in dis mufucka," he said, telling her what she wanted to hear.

Kirby smiled as arrogance filled her head. Her admirer had come out tonight hoping to get his dick wet for the right price. At that moment, Kirby was looking like the perfect prospect. "Why yo' lil' ass got all this?" he slurred, squeezing on her butt. He was fucked up off the dirty Sprite in his Styrofoam cup. "You sexy as hell. But I'm sure I ain't tellin' ya ass shit you don't already know."

Kirby didn't respond as she took his free hand and placed it on her tiny waist. Her admirer had his head rested in the nook of her neck. They were dancing like they came and were leaving together.

Drink a lil' bit...

Smoke a lil' bit...

Pop a lil' bit...

Aye, get fucked up...

Grip's temple throbbed in frustration. He had lost interest in the women in his VIP section, because he was too busy watching Kirby all night. He was already mad that she was kicking it with his uncle. Now he had to watch her dance scantily with some nigga whose first name she didn't know. *I shouldn't even have carried my mufuckin' ass out*, he thought. The only reason he was there was because Castle insisted he turn up since they were in Vegas. The motherfucker lived in the clubs, fronting and showing off like he was a celebrity. Like he was Capone or some shit.

Chill, dawg, Grip told himself. *It ain't like she's yours anyway.* If Kirby were his, he would've crushed dude's skull with his bare hands. He damn sure was capable of it.

"What's your name? I'm Mike."

"Kirby."

"What'chu gettin' into tonight, Ms. Kirby?" he asked. Mike would've paid top dollar to get into her.

"I don't know," she teased.

Mike chuckled. "You playin', ma. Stop flexin'. You know what's up. You feel that shit. I know you do," he said, pushing his dick against her ass.

Apparently, Grip wasn't the only one not feeling the shit. Castle quickly lost interest in his hoes the second he saw Kirby gallivanting with some clown. He took one look at the nigga, and immediately knew he wasn't on his level. *Where she find that fuck nigga?* Castle felt offended and disrespected.

His blood boiled as he watched her dance provocatively.

She was still getting to know Castle, so she wasn't aware of his temper or jealousy. Kirby had the right one. She belonged to him. He'd staked his claim the night he pulled up on her ass, and he was very territorial when it came to his property.

"This young bitch got me fucked up. She tryin' me on some childish shit." Castle didn't like that she was attempting to make him jealous. She was going to fuck around and get somebody killed.

Pushing his way past the birds, Castle approached Kirby with clenched fists. Aviance and Grip immediately noticed that something was up. They knew some shit was about to pop off. Castle had no problem with setting a motherfucker straight, and he didn't give a fuck about being in public. As if on cue, his boys hopped up from their plush VIP chairs and ran over. A full out brawl was on the horizon. And knowing Castle, a murder probably was as well.

6

Castle snatched Kirby away from Mike with such force that he nearly pulled her arm out her socket. The mud he was sipping on had magnified his anger. He got that way anytime he drank lean. Tonight Kirby would learn the very first lesson: don't fuck with him.

"What are you doing?" Kirby asked. She nearly tripped in her heels.

"Aye, man what the fuck?" Mike asked, offended.

Castle shoved the shit out of him. "Nigga, fuck outta here!" he yelled. Castle then turned and rounded on Kirby. "What's in yo' head? Fuck you tryna do, shawty?"

Mike surprised everyone when he shoved Castle back. "Fuck's up, bruh—"

His sentence was cut short after he was bashed him in the mouth with a loaded pistol. Aviance clocked his ass without hesitation. Mike's bottom lip exploded in blood, gushing down his chin and Polo tee. He staggered a bit but somehow managed to maintain his balance.

In a weak attempt to defend himself Mike threw an uncoordinated punch, striking Kirby in the nose.

Grip was the first to retaliate. He swung on Mike with all of his strength, and connected with his jaw. The first hit dropped him instantly. Aviance and the squad immediately joined in, brutally stomping and kicking his body on the floor.

"Nigga, you know who the fuck I am?!" Castle yelled, as Mike was pummeled.

Eyewitnesses backed up in horror. A full out riot had ensued.

Castle turned towards Kirby. There was fear in her big, brown eyes as she held onto her bloody nose. Nothing could've prepared her for this chaos. She'd never been put in that situation before, and a man had never hit her. Although Castle should've consoled her, his anger outweighed his sympathy.

"That's what yo' mufuckin' ass get!" On any other occasion, he would've slapped the shit out of Kirby. He decided to give her a pass since this was her first fuck up. "Grip, get her the fuck outta here, man. Take her back to the hotel. Just get her the fuck out my face," he said dismissively. He didn't even want to look at her ass. She was trying to fuck up his name and reputation, and he couldn't have that shit.

Kirby started to say something in her defense, but Grip grabbed her arm. "Don't touch me!" she hissed, snatching away. Kirby stomped out of the club fuming mad. She was so upset that she could no longer hold back her tears.

Oh boy. Here we go, Grip thought to himself. He had an attitude with her ass too. She had no business even being there and with his uncle, of all people.

Outside Grip found Kirby standing in front of the club with her arms folded. She was definitely having second thoughts about coming to Vegas. Castle had left her with a bad taste in her mouth after tonight.

Instead of asking if she were okay, Grip flagged down valet who promptly brought his truck; a silver G-wagon with matte black custom rims. Kirby was so distracted by what had just happened that she didn't stop to marvel over how nice it was. Hopping in the passenger's seat with an attitude, she slammed the door and yanked on her seatbelt.

"Man, don't be slammin' my door like you crazy, girl. Yo' beef is with *that* nigga. Not with me."

"Whatever, Gavin. Just take me back to the hotel. And give me something for my damn nose."

Grip reached in his middle console for a napkin. "You low-key was askin' for it. You know damn well you shouldn't have been all up in the nigga's face like shit was sweet." He was grilling Kirby like she was his girl. "Yo' ass better be glad Castle ain't leave yo' ass with buddy. I know I would've."

"Just drop it already," Kirby said.

Grip did out of compassion. After several moments of silence, he said, "My fault. Are you good though? Nothin' was cool about what ole boy did."

"I'm good," she stated, dabbing at her nose.

Grip decided it was best he didn't speak since she was in her feelings. The short ride back to the *MGM* was silent. They were two lights away when Kirby decided to finally say something. "So is he always an asshole like that?" she asked. "He came to the club with me, and was talking to other bitches all night like I wasn't even there."

Grip didn't respond. There was no way he would hate on his uncle just to earn cool points. That was some weak shit to do. An awkward silence hung in the air between him and Kirby.

"What he do for a living?" She'd been dying to know since the day they had met. "It's something illegal, right?"

"You in Vegas with a nigga you know nothin' about. What sense does that make?"

Kirby did not expect Grip's brashness. It was like he had something against her after seeing her with Castle. It was clear their relationship had gotten off to a rocky start.

"Does that mean you ain't gon' tell me?" Kirby asked.

Grip kept his attention on the road. She finally became annoyed with his unresponsiveness, and mistook him for having an attitude as well.

"Fine. Don't tell me. I'm just gonna assume it is."

Grip didn't miss the sarcasm in her tone. "You never took me for a chick that was into street niggas anyway," he said. "Just never seemed like ya type. I gotta admit, I was surprised den a mufucka when you walked in with my uncle."

"Why you say that?"

Grip shrugged. "I'on know. You always seemed like a square in school. I picture you with a good guy. Maybe some nigga in college. You know, someone like..."

"You?" Kirby finished his sentence.

Grip scoffed and shook his head. "Ya memory must be foggy. I'm no good guy...but yeah...I guess you could say that. I had wanted yo' ass for a minute, Kirby."

"And then you left. I never heard from or saw you again after that day." Kirby felt odd mentioning the kiss so she didn't.

"It was a lot going on then. My moms passed away," he told her.

Suddenly, Kirby's disposition softened a little—especially considering her own situation. "Wow. I'm sorry to hear that. I really am."

Another awkward silence came to pass.

When they approached a red light, Grip looked over at her. Kirby was cute when she was worked up. He wished he could be there for her all the time like he was tonight. If it were up to him, he would've gone back and whupped on Mike some more.

"You weren't that bad back in the day, Grip," she said. "You weren't a saint, but hell, you did what you had to."

Kirby would never believe the cold-blooded shit his uncle had him doing nowadays. Grip wasn't that same cat she remembered. After losing his parents and catching his first body at 17, Grip would never be that dude again. It was impossible.

Grip pulled his truck in front of the hotel's lobby.

"I wouldn't be surprised if you still stayed in some trouble," she said.

"Shut up and look at me real quick."

Kirby turned to face him, and Grip took a napkin and wiped the dried blood off her cheek.

"I may go back and stomp dat nigga some mo'."

That made Kirby laugh a little.

Grip's thumb lingered on her skin as he lightly caressed her cheek. He was close enough to kiss her. He wanted to like a mothafucka, but he didn't know what type of emotion that would bring about. Tonight Kirby was so hot and cold, and he didn't want to do anything else that might upset her.

Grip was still tempted to suck and nibble on her bottom lip. They were so thick and supple...

"Why you looking at me like that?" Kirby asked him. The smirk in the corner of her mouth let him know that she wasn't too offended.

"Nothin'," he quickly said.

"Well...thanks..." Kirby quickly hopped out and slammed the door behind her. *I just told this girl about slammin' my shit.* Grip could tell she still had an attitude about what happened at the club.

Grip rolled the passenger window down and caught her before she was too far. "Aye, Kirby!" he called out.

She stopped and turned around to face him. "Yeah?" There was a look of agitation on her beautiful face.

Grip hesitated for a second. There were so many things he wanted to say...but couldn't. After finally gathering his thoughts, he asked, "What'chu ever do with that zip I told you to hold?"

Kirby smiled and shook her head. "I gave it to my brother to sell."

***

"I'm surprised your ass ain't out partying. It's type early and you cooped up in the hotel room like you gotta damn curfew."

Kirby FaceTimed McKenzie after the episode in the club, but she refused to tell her friend what happened. It was too embarrassing. Knowing McKenzie she would only find humor out of the situation anyway.

"I do have a curfew. Plus, I didn't feel good," Kirby lied. "But guess who I saw down here though? You ain't gon' believe it. Guess."

"Bitch, do I look psychic? Just tell me."

"You remember Gavin Carmichael? He used to play on the football team."

"Yeah, I remember him. He always stayed in some shit too. Back then, I heard his pops was like Pablo Escobar or some shit."

"I don't know about all that, but why I just find out he's also Castle's nephew?" Kirby withheld the fact that he was also her first kiss.

"Didn't he like you back in the day too?"

"I don't think so. He was always teasing me and stuff. Anyway, how's my mama?" Kirby wanted to change the subject. Tonight, Grip had given her mixed signals. She didn't know what was up with him.

"She's good. Sleeping," McKenzie said. "Anyway, you should be happy I took Marcus off ya hands. The nigga couldn't even fuck *and* he had a little ass dick. Shit was pitiful. A total waste of time. Don't worry though, I changed your sheets."

Kirby's mouth fell open. "Nasty ass bitch. I thought you said you wasn't gonna—" Her voice trailed off after hearing the hotel room door open.

Castle came back sooner than she expected. He and his boys were put out after the violent altercation, and Mike was wheeled off to the hospital.

"Let me hit you back tomorrow," Kirby told McKenzie.

"Bet."

Kirby quickly hung up and waited for him to appear. She was supposed to be enjoying herself with him, but he'd sent her home early like a displeased parent.

Kirby shifted a little in the massive bed to make sure it was Castle walking in. She was still feeling some type of way about how things played out at the club.

Kirby and Castle made brief eye contact before he disappeared inside the bathroom. He didn't even bother speaking. No 'hey', 'wassup', 'are you ok', or anything. She couldn't tell if he was upset with her or not. *Hell, he has no right to be considering the way he acted*, she reasoned. He'd been smiling and feeling up on bitches all night when he was supposed to be there with her. In Kirby's honest opinion, he was just as wrong as she.

When Castle finally emerged from the bathroom, he wore nothing but a pair of black Hanes boxer briefs. Kirby's body instantly betrayed her after her pussy started throbbing. She wanted to be mad still, but she couldn't.

"How's your nose?"

"Better. It stopped bleeding a while ago."

"Don't worry. We fucked that nigga up," he bragged.

Castle climbed in bed with Kirby, and her heart started beating fast. She'd never shared a mattress with a guy before. She almost panicked when he lowered himself at her waist level.

"Why you try me up in the club like that with dat lame ass nigga?" he asked. "You wanted some attention. Huh?" he asked rhetorically. "I know you did. That's the only reason you was doin' that shit. Now you finally 'bout to get some...Open them legs up fuh me..."

Kirby tried to ease back. "Castle, wait—"

Grabbing her waist firmly, he pulled her crotch back towards his face and inhaled. When the tip of his nose brushed against the center of her panties she practically lost it.

Stifling a moan, Kirby whispered, "Castle...hold on...wait—"

"Nah. Fuck that. I hate repeating myself," he said calmly.

Kirby tried to put up a weak struggle, but Castle held her down and ripped her panties off.

"Those were my favorite," she whined.

"Chill. I'll take you shoppin' in the morning."

"Castle, wait...I never—"

"I know. Just relax...Lemme taste it real quick..."

Before Kirby could dispute, Castle lowered his head and flicked his tongue across her juicy clit. She instantly melted at the immense sensation. Kirby had never felt anything more wonderful in life. There was quite a few times when she'd touched herself at night, yet it paled in comparison to the pleasure Castle created.

Kirby's back arched in delight as he expertly kissed, licked, hummed, and sucked on her swollen piece of flesh. Enjoying her reaction, Castle took her hand and placed it on the back of his head. He used his index finger to poke and make sure she was actually a virgin. Kirby winced a little. When he realized she was in fact celibate, his massive dick leaked with pre-cum. He wanted to tear her young ass open, but it was clear she had never even been penetrated. She definitely wasn't ready for 11-inches of uncut thick dick. Instead of popping her cherry that night, he decided to eat the pussy until she quaked and creamed.

Soft whimpers escaped her body as she shivered in ecstasy. Kirby had never experienced anything more blissful. Years of practice had earned Castle a degree in the art of pussy eating.

"This fat ass pussy you got, girl. How you so skinny with this fat ass pussy? Taste good too. I knew you would," he moaned. "You my bitch now, Kirby." Castle placed a trail of delicate kisses along her soft inner thigh. "You hear me? Don't ever try no shit like that again," he told her. "You belong to me."

7

THREE MONTHS LATER...

"Every fucking time...I swear it never fails," Kirby said, shaking her head. She and Castle were supposed to be in a committed relationship, yet every time she went through his phone she found nudes of random bitches. *This nigga acts like he does not have a girlfriend.*

From the bedroom, Kirby could hear the shower water running. Castle had no idea his shit was being investigated. She was quite the detective, and while she was naïve she wasn't crazy. She knew her man had a weakness for bitches, and struggled with keeping his dick in his pants. Just the other day, she found a screenshot of a prostitute's *Backpage* ad in his phone. He was fucking relentless.

Kirby loved Castle, but sometimes she asked herself why she stayed with a nigga who couldn't be faithful. The fact that he was also involved in an organized crime ring made her doubtful they'd have a long future together. He could be killed or imprisoned at any time. On top of that, Castle had involved her by putting houses and cars in her name.

Kirby knew the risk she was taking, but she still allowed it to happen. Three months ago, Castle had moved her and her sick mother down to Atlanta. By then Leah's debilitating illness made her completely bed ridden. She'd given up on chemo, and refused to spend her possibly last days in a cold, boring hospital. Unfortunately, she was too ill to argue about the move.

Kirby, on the other hand, was ecstatic about the move. She thought she could keep a watchful eye on him since they lived together, but she was sadly mistaken.

Castle did whatever the fuck he wanted to, with no regard to her feelings. Despite his unfaithful ways, he took care of her. He put Kirby and her mom up in a beautiful corner unit penthouse in Midtown. He also paid off all of her mother's medical expenses. He even hired a home health aide to care for her.

With her mother sick and her brother in prison, it didn't take long for Kirby to grow extremely close to Castle. She loved him like a companion but admired him like the father figure she never had. He had her so wrapped around his finger, that she didn't realize he'd fucked her head up in the process.

Castle quickly became her world, and they hadn't even fucked yet. She was his bitch regardless. He claimed he would break her in or her 18th birthday, which was next month. The crazy thing was, he'd already raped her young mind. Castle was in her system. He was grooming her to be his loyal ride or die, and in turn, he got faithful pussy from a trained bitch that loved his dirty drawers. It was every nigga's ultimate fantasy.

Castle didn't mind taking care of her in the process. Money wasn't shit. Plus he wanted Kirby to always feel indebted to him. He figured he would achieve more respect and devotion if she always felt like she owed him. He also loved to toss in her face all that he did for her whenever she got out of line. That almost always got her back in check.

Castle had changed Kirby's life for the better and worse. Although he took care of her financially, there was still a heaping of shit buried beneath the glitz and glam. He treated Kirby like crap half the time. He spoke to her however he wanted, came home whenever he felt like it, and fucked whomever he pleased. Kirby had quickly turned from a bright, self-respecting young woman into a damn doormat for him. He'd gotten her while she was too young to realize her potential. Blinded by love, she was unable to see the big picture. Castle was a dog, and he'd always been one.

Kirby's mama always told her "A tiger doesn't change his stripes." All of the wisdom and common sense she'd instilled in her dear daughter seemingly went out the window the moment she laid eyes on him.

"I got somethin' for this mothafucka. I'mma find this bitch," Kirby said to herself.

A fool in love, she took ultimate lows just to have him all to herself. There was no limit to the foul shit she would do in order to make her presence known. She wanted everybody and their mama to know that she was Castle's. Unfortunately, with all of her efforts, it still wasn't enough to make him faithful, and she did not have the courage to leave him.

All of a sudden, Kirby heard the shower water turn off. She knew she had to act fast. After texting herself the nude photos, she posted them for all of her Instagram followers to see. For the caption, she typed *"Name that Nude."* Kirby wanted to know who the skinny bitch with nipple rings was. Social media could be so messy, and she was bound to find out eventually. Someone would surely tag her, or at least an acquaintance of hers. When Kirby finally did find out who she was, come hell or high water, she would track her down. She didn't care if she had to fly to her. She wasn't even the same humble, sweet girl anymore. Castle had created a monster.

Lost in thought, Kirby didn't hear the bathroom door open. Castle emerged from the steamy latrine with a terry cloth towel wrapped around his waist. He took one look at her holding his iPhone and frowned. Kirby was like Sherlock Holmes. "Bitches stay fallin' prey to nosiness", he muttered. "You know that saying about curiosity, right?" Castle threatened. His menacing stare made her nervous, but she held her composure.

"Who is she, Castle?" Kirby demanded to know.

Sucking his teeth, he walked over to the dresser. She had his routine down pact. He'd leave whenever she called him out on his shit, and then come back whenever he felt like it. Only this time, Kirby wouldn't let him off the hook that easily.

"You hear me talkin—"

"Man, Kirby, don't come at me with that childish bullshit," he said. "If you stopped goin' though my phone you'd stop seein' shit you aren't supposed to—"

"You will never change, Castle. I don't why I moved down here and started over with a nigga that can't even be faithful—"

"Bitch, miss me with that same sad ass song." He said with his back to her. "You ain't goin' nowhere and you know it. If it wasn't for me, you'd still be in that roach-infested section 8 ass house in Philly."

"So that makes it okay for you to cheat on me?" Kirby cried. "You told me you wanted to wait 'til I was 18 to have sex...but now I think you're just using that as an excuse to fuck around."

Frustrated with her theatrics, Castle pulled on boxers and a pair of $1800 Balmain jeans. This was what he had to put up with fucking with a teenager. He then pulled a graphic tee over his head, and stepped into a fresh pair of Rick Owens sneakers. "Whatever, Kirby," he said nonchalantly. *She trippin' now, but later a nigga will be back in her good graces after sucking on that lil' pussy.* Castle had her down to a science. Kirby was love drunk off his head game. It was her ultimate weakness, his tool for obtaining forgiveness.

"Why are you always doing this shit? This is the fourth bitch I stumbled across this month! Every time you swear it's the last time, but it never is! You don't even care that you be hurting me—"

"Fuck out my face, Kirby. You startin' to get on my damn nerves," he told her. "Sometimes you really tempt a nigga to pack up ya shit and send you back to where you came from. You ain't ready for no real nigga."

Castle loved to turn the tables on her whenever an argument broke out. He also threatened to "deport her" whenever she stepped out of line. She was so used to hearing it that she wasn't even phased by his words.

Kirby, still determined to get answers, snatched the phone off the bed and thrust it in his face. She wanted Castle to get a good look at the tasteless nude photo. "WHO IS SHE?"

Whap!

Castle slapped the phone out of Kirby's hand. "Get that fucking shit out my face."

Kirby quickly knelt down to retrieve it, but he stepped on her hand before she could.

"Don't touch my shit," he snarled. "Next time I catch you in my phone, I'mma break ya fuckin' fingers."

Kirby yelped in pain. If Castle didn't lift his foot soon, he was sure to crush her hand.

"You hear me?"

"Get the fuck off my hand!"

Castle ignored her. "I asked you a fuckin' question, lil' girl. Do you hear me?" he repeated. He paused between each word for added emphasis.

"Yes!" Kirby cried out.

Satisfied with her response, he finally removed his foot and watched as she cradled her hand. Castle slowly bent down and grabbed his iPhone. "Ass got no business in my shit no way," he mumbled.

Castle didn't bother apologizing as he grabbed his wallet and stormed out. Kirby would have to learn the hard way. She would never be able to tame or control a man like him.

8

"Man, stop fuckin' tryin' to control me, McKenzie!" Aviance yelled. He'd flown down to Philadelphia in hopes of spending time with his girl without the headache. The 20-year old was getting everything but hospitality from McKenzie. Since he had landed, she'd been giving him nothing but grief, attitude and lip.

They were supposed to be chilling and watching Netflix, but an argument somehow erupted the minute she didn't get her way. The two met three months ago when she flew down to Atlanta to help Kirby get settled in, and they'd been kicking it heavy ever since.

"How is me wanting to be closer to you controlling—"

"Don't fuckin' play with me. I know what'chu on, man. You only tryin' to move down to Atlanta so you can keep tabs on a nigga. I told you I ain't with that shit, McKenzie," he stressed. "What we got is cool. We straight. Why fuck it up or add unnecessary pressure?"

Aviance was a handsome, light-skinned brotha with chinky eyes and thick lips. He too was bi-racial with a headful of curly jet-black hair he wore in a fro with tapered sides. Tatted in bold lettering on the side of his neck was RBM. He lived and would die for the mafia.

Aviance's track record with women was as bad as McKenzie's was with men, but they balanced each other out. She never found out that he'd tried to get with her girl first.

"Castle moved Kirby down South!" McKenzie argued.

Her face was beet red with anger. She was used to getting her way with men most of the time...but Aviance was far from being most men. He was the only nigga able to handle her spoiled, bratty ass. The only man capable of taming a girl whose reputation preceded her. Aviance heard the rumors about her being thottish, but he still didn't give a fuck. Even though McKenzie was a handful half the time, he had love for her.

Aviance never had an official girlfriend. McKenzie definitely was the closest thing to it, though he still did his shit on the side.

Ever since Castle moved Kirby down south, she'd been hassling Aviance about doing the same. He wasn't feeling the idea at all. He'd rather she attended college or pursue some type of venture. Instead, all she wanted to do was fuck and lay up under a trap nigga while secretly competing with her best friend.

Aviance was tired of McKenzie comparing their relationship to Castle and

Kirby's. He didn't need that extra pressure. He did his best to keep her content, but sometimes it felt like it wasn't enough. McKenzie was so distracted by her pursuit of happiness, that she hardly paused just to enjoy being happy.

"How many times I gotta remind yo' ass, McKenzie? We not Castle and muhfuckin' Kirby! Stop comparin' us to them! The shit's annoying."

"You right! We sure as shit ain't them," she snorted. "Castle and Kirby down there living like Jay and Bey."

Aviance chuckled and shook his head. McKenzie didn't know the half of it. It was so easy to assume when you were on the outside looking in. "Oh yeah? And what does that make us then?" he asked out of curiosity.

McKenzie waved him off. "A fake ass Nicki and Meek."

Aviance broke out laughing at the funny comparison. McKenzie was always acting like he never did shit for her, because it wasn't as grand or ostentatious as the things Castle did for Kirby.

"Man, you somethin' else, Freckles," he laughed.

Aviance had given her the nickname back when they first started dating. He didn't even bother reminding her that he'd put her in the apartment she lived in. McKenzie bitched so much about living with her mama that he finally moved her out a couple months back. The 2011 Honda she pushed was also compliments of his hustle. Instead of appreciating Aviance for all that he did, she hounded him for more.

McKenzie wanted the fancy cars and penthouses like her friend had. She was so hell-bent on keeping up with Kirby, that she'd allowed herself to become jealous. Castle moved Kirby out of the hood to the good life. It wasn't fair that she be the one left behind.

"I'm serious," she said. "Don't you ever feel like you want more?"

"Of course I do—"

"Well...you never considered maybe...*taking* the throne?" McKenzie hinted.

Aviance did an automatic double take. For a second, he thought his ears were deceiving him. He almost didn't believe the shit spewing from McKenzie's lips. "What the fuck are you talkin' 'bout?" He knew damn well what she was getting at, but he wanted to be sure he wasn't tripping.

"You've been working for that motherfucker since you were thirteen. You've put in more than your fair share of work—"

"Are you sayin' that I should set my nigga up? Have you lost yo' fuckin' mind,

McKenzie? See, I knew I should've never started telling yo' ass 'bout the business!"

"I'm just saying. The nigga be flexin' like he your uncle and shit but pays you pennies. You should be pushing Maseratis. You should be living in mansions. You be doing all the hard work. All that nigga do is sit back and tell ya'll what the fuck to do. Think about it," she said. "With his product you can start your own business and get off the block—"

Aviance quickly cut her off. "There ain't shit to think about! I can't 'een believe I'm hearin' you right now. You talkin' crazy, yo!" He jumped up off the couch in an attempt to put some much needed space between them.

"No, I'm making all the sense in the world. You just can't fucking handle it," McKenzie stated. "I swear you be frontin' like you so hard, but softer than fucking Kleenex. With that hand me down ass jewelry you be wearin'. Don't think I don't know Castle be givin' you that shit once he's bored with it."

Aviance waved her off. "Whatever, man. I'm out. I ain't finna sit here and listen to this bullshit." Grabbing his phone and car keys, he headed to the front door. He had to get the hell away from McKenzie before he did or said something he might regret.

"So you gon' leave? Just like that?" McKenzie yelled. She quickly hopped up and ran after him. She was the first one to talk shit, but never wanted Aviance to go. The young couple shared a love-hate relationship, and yet they couldn't leave the other alone.

McKenzie tried to grab his forearm on the way out the door, but he violently snatched away.

"Fuck it then! Leave! Walk away like a lil' pussy!" she yelled down the hall. McKenzie didn't care that the building's walls were paper-thin. Every tenant probably heard her shouting like a banshee. "You'll never be a nigga in charge, Aviance! You too busy being Castle's lil' lap dog! Whenever that nigga says jump you jump. As long as you work for that mothafucka you'll always be a puppet on strings!"

"Fuck you, McKenzie," he shot over his shoulder.

Lingering in the doorway of her apartment, McKenzie fought back tears. She wanted to be honest, but not at the cost of running him away. "Aviance, I'm sorry. Please come back."

Aviance didn't stop or turn around for McKenzie. Her ass needed time alone so she could sit and think about what she'd said. "Nah, not this time. I'm done with'cha ass. I put that on everything."

In silence, McKenzie watched him disappear inside the elevator. He was talking that shit now, but she knew he'd be back. Aviance could never stay away for too long.

***

Femi and Monica were in her kitchen when her husband finally walked in. Monica didn't even bother greeting him as she helped herself to his bag of BBQ chips. She needed something to hold her over while Femi prepared supper. Monica ate dinner over their house damn near every day like she was apart of the family. She had no kids, no man, and no life. She was constantly teased about it, but she never made an effort to change things. She claimed things were fine just the way they were.

"Well, well, well. Look what the cat dragged in." Femi curled her lip up as soon as her husband walked up.

She was the only woman fully capable of taking his shit. Femi had held him down through everything; prison, poverty. She'd even sold the pussy a couple times for him just to make ends meet. Femi would forever remain wifey. Regardless of everything she'd done and sacrificed for him, he still indulged.

Castle was so damn predictable. The motherfucker popped up whenever he felt like it with a different bitch's scent on him every day of the week. After fifteen years, his routine hadn't changed.

"Why you got these lil' hoes playing on my girl's phone?" Monica chimed in. She loved putting herself in the middle of their business since she didn't have any of her own. "And what's this about you getting some bitch pregnant?" Monica was going off on his ass like she was his wife.

"What the fuck is she talkin' 'bout now?" Castle asked. He never really cared for Monica or her big mouth. She needed a life and to stay the fuck out of his. "You's a dummy. You back pumpin' my wife's head up with nonsense?"

"I don't think a child is nonsense. Do you, Femi?"

Castle wanted to slap the potato chip crumbs off her face. She was forever instigating, and he hated the shit.

"Some bitch called my phone claiming you knocked her up a few months back. For your sake, I hope she's fucking lying." Femi told him.

"Bitches story-tell all the time. I ain't get no bitch pregnant," he said. "Stop listenin' to these lyin', hatin' ass hoes." Castle specifically looked over in Monica's direction.

"It's hard not to when you got a different one calling my girl every week," Monica piped up.

"How 'bout you get'cho ass out my crib 'fore I put yo' big ass out," he threatened.

Monica looked over at Femi who quickly looked away. As usual, she never came to her friend's rescue whenever it involved her husband. She never liked to get in the middle of their shit. Besides, she could manage Castle on her own.

Grabbing her Michael Kors bag off the counter, Monica stormed out of the kitchen with an attitude.

"Fuck is she on?" Castle asked once he heard the front door slam.

"She's every bit of right," Femi said, folding her arms. "I need to know if you really got that bitch pregnant...cuz if you did Castle I swear—"

"Why you believe that dumb shit, huh?"

Femi didn't answer right away. Instead, she looked him dead in the eyes to see if she could detect bullshit. She would've left him a long time ago if it wasn't for the prenuptial and the fact that she still loved him. Castle was a dog, but she'd given up on trying to change him. Her grandmother always told her 'you can't teach an old dog new tricks.' Pushing thirty-seven, Castle was already set and stuck in his trifling ass ways.

"Because I know you, Castle...Better than any fucking body does," she told him.

At 16, Femi had gotten knocked up and the rest was history. She could remember struggling right alongside Castle as he and his brother made their come up. Femi put in her fair share of work, and earned her crown as queen. She even participated in Benny's set up. Femi was the real MVP—an unquestionable ride-or-die. There was once a time when she would've given her life for Castle. Hell, she would've taken a rap for him if that meant keeping him out of prison. She would've done anything for her husband. Now Femi was just settling, because he was all that she knew.

"Apparently, you don't if you think I'd do some fucked up shit like that. You really believe I'd get a square bitch out here knocked up? Fuck I look like?"

"You tell me. You the one that's always in the streets."

"Don't start that shit, Femi. I be workin'."

"*Unh-huh*, yeah. Sure you do," she said. "Did you get that bitch pregnant or not, Castle? Be real. I can't take any more of the fucking lies."

"Man, I ain't been fuckin' no bitches—"

"Don't insult my intelligence, Castle. I been with your ass for fifteen years. The least you can do is look me in the eyes and tell me you didn't get that hoe pregnant. Tell me you didn't have me tie my gotdamn tubes just so you could make babies with side bitches—"

"Man, gon' head with that bullshit, Femi! I had you do the shit 'cuz the birth control was makin' ya pussy dry! I ain't got no mufuckin' hoes pregnant 'cuz I ain't been fuckin' nobody!"

"Bullshit!" Femi shoved him in anger. "The bitch was texting me pictures of ya'll together! What are you gonna say next? They were Photo shopped?! Stop fucking lying, Castle! And how the fuck does she know about the tubectomy? You be telling these hoes my business too? How the fuck could you do that to me, Castle—"

"I don't be telling nobody shit. Man, people talk, Femi, and a lot of mufuckas know me. I don't know what the fuck you want me to say?"

"I want you to look me in the face and tell me you didn't get that bitch pregnant!" There were tears in Femi's eyes. She wouldn't know what to do with herself if he did. It would've been the ultimate betrayal.

"On my soul, I ain't get no bitches pregnant!" Castle hollered. Truthfully, he did impregnate Trina, but what she failed to tell Femi was that he forced her to get an abortion. She simply wanted to get under his wife's skin since she knew that she was sterile. "Can't believe you even comin' at me with this bullshit," he said angrily. "A nigga ain't been home in weeks, and this the fuckin' greeting I get? I may as well just bounce. Ain't like you fuckin' with me."

Castle started to walk out of the kitchen, but Femi grabbed his wrist. She hated his prolonged absence. "Don't you fucking walk out of here," she said. "Since you ran my guest off, I need a dinner date..." Just like that all of Femi's hatred towards him dissipated. That was exactly how their relationship went; a typical case of 'can't live with him, can't live without him'.

Pleased with her acquiescence, Castle kissed the side of his wife's neck, causing her to shiver in response. "I'd rather eat you for dinner."

"Whatever."

"You missed me?"

Femi placed her arms around his neck while gazing lovingly into his chestnut eyes. He wasn't shit half the time, but she loved him tremendously. Castle was all that she knew. "And what if I did?" Femi asked. "It won't matter. It's not like if I say yes, you'll stay home more."

Castle looked around at the beautiful state-of-the-art kitchen they were standing in. "Aye, you love this lifestyle, don't you?"

"I love you more, Castle. I always have."

Castle sighed deeply and looked away. "I can't slow down, babe. You know that."

"How many?" Femi asked him.

"How many what?"

"How many millions do you have to make before you finally decide to slow down?"

Castle pretended to mull over her question. "I'll retire when I'm dead..."

Femi shook her head and forced a smile. She wanted to argue with him. She wanted to remind him of their net worth, but it wouldn't have done a damn thing in the end. Castle was a hustler. Who was she to take that away from him?

"Where's my baby girl?" Castle asked. He hadn't seen his 16-year old daughter in a few days, and he was past due to check up on her.

"Princess is upstairs in her room."

Castle gently cupped Femi's chin, and kissed her with the same passion as their wedding day. She longed for those days, but she knew things would never go back to how they used to be. It was simply wishful thinking.

"I love you," he said. Castle stared deeply into her hazel eyes. He wasn't perfect by a long shot but Femi loved him like he was flawless.

"I love you too."

"Turn around, let me see dat fat ass. Feels like I ain't seen dat mufucka in forever."

Femi giggled as she turned around and let him squeeze on her booty. "I'mma drop this dick in you tonight. You can believe dat shit," he said. Castle pecked her a final time, before walking off towards his daughter's bedroom. Unlike Femi, he never knocked upon entering, and Princess didn't expect her father to just barge in.

The young nigga in her bed quickly jumped up in surprise. His jeans were undone; from the looks of it shit was getting pretty hot and heavy.

"The fuck?"

"Daddy, it's not what it looks like!" Princess pled.

Castle wasn't trying to hear any of that shit. Without thinking twice, he snatched the pistol off his hip and walked up on the young punk. "You let this mufucka in our house?! In yo' bed! Have you lost yo' gotdamn mind?"

"Daddy, please—I swear we weren't doing anything," Princess lied.

"So this nigga just walks around everyday with his mufuckin' pants unbuckled, huh? What do you think? I'm fuckin' stupid or some shit?"

Princess's boyfriend, Tony held his hands up in surrender. "Sir, with all due respect, I—"

WHAM!

Castle brutally hit him in the nose with the butt of his gun. The force of the blow was strong enough to break it. Blood poured from his nostrils and seeped into his mouth. He wasn't expecting Castle to fly off the handle. Unfortunately, he had no idea who Princess's father was or what he was capable of.

"DADDY, NO!!" she cried.

After hearing all the noise, Femi ran upstairs and stopped in the doorway. "Castle, what are you doing?!"

"Did you know she had some fuck nigga up here in her room?" he hollered.

Tony said a silent prayer as he held onto his broken nose. His face was slowly beginning to swell. He needed a hospital and badly.

"Yes, I knew, Castle. I gave her permission to have company—"

"*Company*? Is you fuckin' crazy, bitch? You let some nigga make himself comfortable in *MY* home?!" he yelled. "The place where *I* pay all the mufuckin' bills? You must've slipped and bumped yo' fuckin' head!"

"Castle, she's sixteen! You gotta cut the umbilical cord already. We can't keep a leash on her forever—"

Femi's sentence was cut short when he slapped the shit out of her. Princess shrieked and covered her mouth in horror. She'd only seen her father hit her mother once in life, and she was just a kid then.

Tony had no idea what he'd just walked into.

Femi grabbed her stinging cheek while fighting to not look embarrassed. She'd underestimated her husband's temper, and now she was paying for it. Had she known he was coming home today, she would have never agreed to it. "I'm sorry," she told Tony. "I...you should leave."

Castle pointed his gun at the teenage boy. "You heard her. Yo' ass got five seconds to get the fuck on or I'm squeezin', lil' nigga."

The poor guy didn't even need three as he fled the room with his life still intact.

"You didn't have to do that, daddy—"

"Shut the fuck up, Princess. Shut yo' fuckin' mouth right now before I slap you. I don't wanna hear shit yo' ass got to say. Matter fact, gimme ya phone."

Princess stubbornly did as she was told. Her phone was her lifeline.

Castle could see the resentment in her eyes. He didn't care if she hated him. In the end, all he wanted to do was protect her. He loved Princess, and he wasn't about to watch her become the bitches he fucked. Pointing a finger at his daughter he said, "Next time you have some nigga in my house, I won't hesitate to kill the mufucka. Remember that shit."

9

After an awkwardly silent dinner with his wife and daughter, Castle headed out to the pool where he lit up an L. Femi hated whenever he smoked in the house because she complained the smell lingered.

Castle let her pick out the six-bedroom home 4 years ago. Although he wasn't husband of the year, there wasn't shit he wouldn't do for Femi. She was his queen, and while he loved her with every fiber of his being, he couldn't help indulging every now and again. Castle loved bitches. He needed the pussy and attention like a person needed oxygen. It fueled him; it was something his wife would never be able to understand.

Since he was alone, Castle decided to call up his second favorite girl. Kirby answered on the third ring; she was obviously missing a nigga. "Where are you, Castle? Come home," she insisted.

"I'm still mad at yo' ass."

"I'm mad at you too, but I don't wanna fight no more, Castle. Come home."

All of a sudden, he heard movement behind him. "I'll think about it. Lemme hit you back," he quickly said before hanging up. Castle thought it was Femi walking up on him, but it was actually his 2-year old English bulldog, Diesel.

"Aye, wassup, boy?" Castle knelt down and scratched behind his ear. After ashing the blunt, he slowly made his way back inside the home. He found Femi in their master bedroom suite making the bed.

Castle didn't speak to her right away. He thought about staying the night with one of his freaks, but knew how much Femi missed him. That was probably the only reason she hadn't gone postal about Trina.

"You still ain't talking to me?" Femi asked. "You hate me?"

Castle pulled his shirt off and climbed in bed. "I don't hate you. I just ain't fuckin' wit'cho ass right now. You knew better than to have some nigga in my crib."

"I'm sorry, Castle." Femi scooted over next to him and snuggled close. "If I would've known it'd make you that upset, I would've never agreed to it." She gently took his hand and slid his index finger in her warm mouth. "Let me make it up to you..."

Castle's dick immediately sprang to life. Finally, she was talking his language. "Gon' head then. Bounce on this big mufucka and we'll call it even."

***

The following afternoon, Kirby took *Uber* to Grip's loft in Castleberry Hills. Because of their mutual acquaintances, they'd quickly gotten closer over a short period. As a matter of fact, Kirby spent more leisure time with Grip than with her own man. Whenever McKenzie came in town, they all hung and went out together. There were even a few occasions when people said they were a cute couple even though they were just friends.

Kirby wouldn't admit it, but she was far more compatible with Grip than Castle. They were closer in age, and she felt like she could relate to him better. Castle was seventeen years her senior, so his mentality was way different than hers.

With Grip, she felt as if she could be herself without looking or sounding childish. Whenever they were together, they talked about everything; movies, music, TV shows, and the best memories from their high school days. If it wasn't for the fact that he lived in Atlanta, Kirby might've gone stir crazy without a friend.

When Kirby finally arrived at Grip's loft, she let herself in with the spare key he'd given her. Fortunately, Castle didn't know about that. He already thought the two were uncomfortably too chummy. "Honey, I'm home!" she playfully sang.

Grip appeared from the back of the loft wearing nothing but a pair of gray sweatpants. Kirby had to stop herself from staring too hard at his bulging muscles. She could see the imprint of his curved dick through the cotton fabric. Grip spent most of his free time in the boxing gym and it definitely paid off immensely.

"Keep lookin' at me like that, and I'mma fuck ya lil' ass, Kirby."

She quickly tore her gaze away from his amazing physique. "Whatever, Grip. You ready for me to re-twist your dreads? You got all the shit, right?" she asked. Kirby had learned to maintain dreads after her brother got his.

"Yup."

Kirby followed Grip into his massive living room with high ceilings. His golden Irish wolfhound was seated in the corner of the room atop a doggy lounger.

"You talked to Castle recently? He avoiding me like the plague right now," she said.

"Not in a couple days," he replied.

"Yesterday I found another nudie in his phone," she told him.

Grip had to stop himself from telling her he didn't give a fuck. "That's nothing new," he simply said.

Kirby pulled out her phone and showed him the pic. "I posted it on my Instagram. I'm waiting on somebody to comment or DM me her address."

"You petty as fuck, Kirby. Don't expect a co-sign from me. You dead wrong for that foul shit."

"And so is he!" Kirby said in her defense.

Grip snatched her iPhone and tossed it on the nearby sofa. "Fuck that bullshit for a minute. I need all your attention on me." He picked her up and sat her down on the love seat before plopping in between her legs.

"You washed your hair first?" Kirby asked, running her fingers through his scalp. His roots were soft because of the good texture he'd inherited from his mom. His hair was so fine that a few of his dreadlocks were twisted together.

A low groan escaped Grip's throat. He loved for his scalp to be massaged. He could fall asleep with Kirby doing that shit. "Marissa washed it yesterday," he said with his eyes closed.

"Who's Marissa?" Kirby asked. Her tone was laced with jealousy; this was the first time she'd heard the name.

"A friend."

Kirby grunted, and Grip got a kick out of knowing that she cared enough to ask.

After moisturizing, re-twisting, and blow-drying his dreads, Kirby playfully mushed his head to let him know she was done. "That'll be $2000," she said with her hand outstretched.

Grip grabbed her hand and pulled her down onto the floor with him. Kirby tried to wrestle with him, but she was no match against his 6"3 frame. They were forever horse playing like a pair of kids.

After pinning Kirby down, Grip slid in between her legs. Her maxi dress was hiked up and she could feel his erection pressing against her inner thigh. "I'd rather repay you with somethin' else..."

"Move, Grip!" Kirby laughed. He was making her nervous, and he knew it.

Grip ignored her pleas as he kept her pinned underneath his body. "Is he hittin' it yet?"

"Grip—"

"Answer the fuckin' question."

"No."

"Lemme poke it."

Kirby howled with laughter and tried to push him off. It was like trying to move a 2-ton boulder. She couldn't have been more than 120 lbs. soaking wet. "Move! Let me go, Grip!"

"I don't wanna let you go," he said, gazing in her eyes. "I wanna keep you."

"You can't..."

"Why?" he asked. "Why I can't have you? Tell me why I can't have you, Kirby."

"You know why, Grip."

"We keep fuckin' 'round like this, and I'mma have to take you."

Kirby gently touched his stubble. She would be lying to herself if she said she wasn't attracted to Grip. His muscular build, his black and gold dreads, his tattoos, and the faint dimple in his chin...he was everything...but he was also her man's nephew.

Grip leaned in close like he was about to kiss her. He'd quickly forgotten that she was off limits.

"I honestly don't think we should be doing this, Grip," she whispered. "You know I'm with Castle..."

"...I honestly don't give a fuck..."

Grip was just about to go in for the kiss when he suddenly heard someone walk in the room.

10

"GOTEEM!"

Grip quickly climbed off Kirby once Aviance moseyed in the living room. Unfortunately, he didn't move fast enough. His boy also had a key to his crib. They'd been caught red-handed in the act.

Wearing a knowing grin, Aviance looked from Kirby to Grip. He always thought there was something funny going on between them, and now he knew it for a fact. "Don't try to get decent now. Ya'll mufuckas ain't slick," he chuckled.

"We weren't doin' shit. She just got done twistin' a nigga up," Grip told him.

"*Unh-huh.* Whatever you say, chief." Aviance plopped down on a sofa and kicked his feet up on the glass coffee table like he paid rent. He then looked down next to him and saw Kirby's cellphone. Aviance wanted to go through her IG to see what new female friends she'd made, but instead he got an eyeful of the tasteless nude photo.

"Who the fuck is this?" he asked, holding up her iPhone.

Kirby stood to her feet and straightened her dress out. "I don't know. You may wanna ask Castle," she said. "I found it in his phone the other day. I swear the nigga has more naked pics than Fuckbook."

Aviance laughed. "Hell nah. How yo' lil' ass know about Fuckbook?"

"'Cuz the mothafucka had an account behind my back," she told him.

"Gotdamn."

"Relentless, ain't he?" Kirby agreed.

"Get'chu an ugly nigga," Aviance told her. "Ugly niggas is winnin'."

"Don't get her fucked up," Grip chimed in. He didn't like the sound of her making new male friends. He'd have to hem a nigga up over Kirby.

Aviance held his hands up in mock surrender. He definitely wasn't trying to start any shit between them. It was obvious that Grip had become possessive of her.

"What'cho ass doin' here anyway, nigga?"

"Just copped that new Madden '16." Aviance tossed the unopened video game on the glass table. "And I got that new pack." He pulled a 7 from his pocket and placed it next to the game. "You tryna get ya ass whupped before you slide, Kirbz?"

"Um. I'll pass. I gotta meet McKenzie at the airport."

Aviance was unmoved by the unexpected visit. He still wasn't speaking to her spoiled ass.

"McKenzie told me to tell you to stop ignoring her calls and texts."

"Man, fuck McKenzie. I ain't fuckin' with that bitch right now."

"Aye, I'm just the messenger."

"I'mma walk you to the door then," Grip offered.

Aviance popped the video game in the Xbox One and proceeded to roll up. They were positive that he wouldn't tell a soul about what he saw. Grip and Aviance had been boys for over two years. The day they met they clicked instantly. Some of the niggas in the mob even teased Aviance by calling him Grip's sidekick.

"Text me. Lemme know you made it in safe once you get ya girl."

"I will."

Kirby was about to walk off, but Grip grabbed her dress and pulled her close. "I was serious about what I said. Don't be cheatin' on me or shit gon' get bad. And I mean that. If you fuck him, I'mma fuck you up."

"Whatever. Bye, Grip. You just worry about Marissa."

***

School had just let out and Princess was still feeling some type of way about the stunt her father pulled yesterday—especially since Tony didn't show up for classes. After parking her pink Mercedes Benz convertible, she slammed the door and stomped through the baby mansion. She was determined to give him a piece of her mind when she stormed inside her parents' bedroom. Unfortunately, her mother was the only one occupying the bed.

Castle had dicked her down so good last night that she slept well into the afternoon. Her phone had a dozen text messages and missed calls from Monica.

"Ma, that was fucked up what dad did! Tony didn't even come to school today. I hope he presses charges on his crazy ass."

Femi wiped the sleep residue from her eyes and stared at her twin. Princess was a spitting image of her minus the attitude. Sometimes she thought Princess inherited that from Monica. She'd been around since before she was born and had a heavy influence in her goddaughter's life.

"What time is it?"

"Time for you to divorce that maniac. He be doing too damn much and you know it. The bitches, the temper, the FBI agents that's always lurking around our house, I'm sick of it! I'm sick of him! What he did to my boyfriend was the last straw!"

"You know how your father is."

"I don't care how he is! Nothing was normal about what he did yesterday. He broke Tony's nose!"

"You shouldn't have had him in your bed, Princess."

"And you shouldn't have had a kid and married a psychotic drug dealer. UGH! I hate my fucking life! I'd be happier being an orphan with a cleft lip somewhere in a third world country."

"Stop being so damn dramatic, girl."

"Are you gonna say something to him about it or not?" Princess asked. She would never tell her mom that she and Tony planned on dumping the house's safe so they could run away together. Femi may've been cool putting up with Castle's shit, but he could kiss her black ass. Once they left Georgia, he would never see or hear from her again.

"You know there's no changing Castle's outlook on certain things..."

Defeated, Princess sucked her teeth and left the room in a huff. "Pessimistic bitch," she mumbled on her way out.

***

"Mail call!"

Every inmate in their pod practically flocked to the female correctional officer carrying the box of envelopes. Those days were like Christmas for the prisoners.

Kaleb, on the other hand, wasn't too hopeful for a letter from anyone. McKenzie was the only person who wrote him nowadays and half the time he didn't even bother opening them shits. He had a stack of envelopes addressed from her piling up in the corner of his cell like they were bills. She'd been crazy in love with his ass since middle school.

Kaleb was the epitome of a pretty boy. Standing at an average 5"9, he had even-toned cinnamon-colored skin with hazel eyes and the deepest set of dimples. Much like his sister, he was slender in frame but kept himself in shape by doing push ups and running laps every day. The dreads that once touched the center of his back had been cut due to prison regulations, now he wore a tapered fade.

Kaleb was a real bad ass, but the ladies loved him—and he was far from being the most charismatic nigga. That much was evident when he pinched the CO's ass after she walked past. He was standing in the doorway of his cell, leaned against the frame when she switched by. It was recreational time in his pod, but he didn't politic with the other inmates. The only cat he fucked with was the ole' head he shared a cell with.

"Aye, wassup with that top?" he asked, licking his lips. Kaleb had been fucking two of the female correctional officers during his stay. He had one who religiously put money on his books using an alias, and another who blessed him with head every time they had a chance to be alone.

Karen smirked and strutted past him in her form-fitting uniform. She wasn't the prettiest woman, but beggars couldn't be choosers when you were locked up. Besides, pussy was pussy.

"Inmate, distance," she warned him. Because of the grin on her lips, he didn't take her too seriously. Those same lips would be wrapped around his dick during recess. "Oh, wait. I actually got one for you, Kaleb."

He was just about to walk back in his cell when she stopped and turned around. Kaleb stared strangely at the letter she handed him. It was addressed from his mother but it wasn't Leah's handwriting.

Grabbing the envelope, Kaleb slowly walked over to the bunk and sat on the bottom mattress. The letter started off with Leah explaining that she had her caregiver write it for her. She filled him in on the status of her debilitating health and everything that'd been going on in her and Kirby's life, including the move.

Kaleb's grip tightened on the paper after reading about the womanizing 36-year old nigga his sister was dating. Leah told him all about Castle, and how he'd gotten comfortable dogging and putting his hands on Kirby.

"Man, who the fuck's this nigga?" Kaleb asked in disgust. He blamed himself for Kirby's downfall. If he weren't incarcerated she wouldn't have ended up with some clown. He'd be the one taking care of her and mom. Kaleb had to get his little sister away from that mothafucka.

"Everything good?" his roommate Rodney asked. He was on his second set of sit-ups. At 57 he was exceptionally fit for his age. The last thing he wanted was to not be able to protect himself in the zoo they called prison. He'd been slapped with a life sentence after murdering a police officer during a raid.

"Nah...but it will be soon," Kaleb told him. Luckily, his release date was approaching. In the meantime, he would write back to both his mother and McKenzie. He wanted to know everything there was to know about Kirby's new love interest. Kaleb couldn't wait to get at that nigga Castle.

11

"Damn. Can we walk with ya'll?" a cute dark-skinned guy with cornrows asked.

Kirby and McKenzie were traipsing through *Lenox Square* when a trio of fellas approached them. Kirby was dressed casually that day in jeans and a cream crop top, while McKenzie wore a too short heather gray dress that hugged her body.

"It depends. Ya'll trying to buy our fits for tonight?" McKenzie boldly replied.

All of a sudden, they weren't so interested.

"Kirby?"

Hearing her name, she turned around and noticed Grip staring awkwardly at her from a distance. He didn't look too pleased by the sight of the guys she was talking to. As soon as they saw the intimidating 6"3 disciplinarian, they dispersed immediately. A nigga didn't need those types of problems.

"Who the fuck was them niggas?" he asked, approaching her. The scowl on his handsome face indicated his territorialism. One would've assumed she was his girl.

"Nobody."

"Don't get these mufuckin' niggas out here assaulted, Kirby," he warned her.

"Why it matter who she talks to? What'chu gon' do? Report to Castle?" McKenzie asked sarcastically.

"Why you in my mouth when I ain't talkin' to yo' ass?" Grip countered.

"Relax. I'm only fucking with you," McKenzie said after realizing he wasn't joking. "Aviance ain't with you?" she asked, looking over his shoulder.

"Nah, he ain't."

"What's up? What are you doing here?" Kirby asked him. They just so happened to be at *Lenox Square Mall* at the same time. Grip looked sexy in khaki shorts, a Givenchy tee, and Balenciaga sneakers. His long dreads were tied back, and a cloud of Creed fragrance surrounded him. The Cartier on his wrist sparkled, right along with the golds in his mouth.

Kirby was surprised to see him alone. Whenever they did cross paths he was almost always with Aviance, or one of the niggas from the Mafia.

"Just kickin' shit. What's happenin' wit'chu?"

Kirby tried to pretend she didn't notice how attractive he was. Her mind drifted back to their first kiss, and the recent moment they shared at his loft. Grip was fine and she liked that he seemed low-key. He was the complete opposite of his obnoxious ass uncle. Still, Kirby loved him unconditionally, and because of that, she quickly shook the dangerous thoughts from her mind. Grip was Castle's nephew. There was no way they could ever be together.

"Nothing much. Have you seen or talked to Castle today?" she asked. "He ain't answering my calls, and he ain't been home in a couple days."

Kirby still thought she was special. What she didn't know was that Castle had a plethora of hoes, some of which he'd put up in houses as well. Kirby wasn't any fucking exception. Grip just hated that she didn't know it yet.

He truly felt sorry for Kirby. She had no clue of what she was up against. "Shit, you know how my uncle is," he simply said. "And ain't it your job to keep tabs on him. I'm tired of you always pressin' me 'bout where he is whenever you see a nigga." Grip was pissed that she'd even fix her mouth up to ask him some shit like that. She knew how a nigga felt about her.

"Damn. Someone got hostile quick," McKenzie butted in. "Chill. It was just a simple question, Grip."

"A simple question she need to be askin' another mufucka. I don't clock that nigga's moves." There was no way in hell he'd tell Kirby that Castle was probably laid up with his wife or one of his many other side bitches.

"Well, you work for him. So it's kinda your job to keep up with him too."

"Exactly. I work for him. Not you. That's yo' man. If you wanna know where he is, go find the nigga."

He missed the days when Kirby didn't know about the business at all. Apart of him felt obligated to tell her the truth but he couldn't contest with blood. Kirby would just have to find out for herself.

All of a sudden, a cute light-skinned chick walked up and looped her arm around his. "Hey bay. I thought you were gonna wait for me. I told you I wasn't gonna be long."

A twinge of jealousy gnawed at Kirby. *Who the hell is this bitch*? She wondered if it was his girl or the infamous Marissa. Seeing him with a random chick definitely had her feeling some type of way.

"Aye, I'mma get up with ya'll later. It was good seeing you, Kirby and good luck in ya search."

Kirby didn't miss the sarcasm in his voice. She forced herself to mumble, "You too," just to keep the peace between them. As she walked away, Kirby couldn't help but wonder if that was his woman. "Why Grip ain't introduce his girl to us?" she asked McKenzie.

Her friend shrugged like it was no big deal. "Why it matter?" McKenzie still didn't know about their mutual attraction, so she didn't get why Kirby cared.

Maybe they aren't that serious, Kirby thought. *Listen to me. And so what if they are. Grip is not my nigga. I shouldn't even give a damn who he fucks with. It's not my business.*

Kirby was saying one thing, but the envy in her heart said another. Truth be told, she didn't enjoy seeing Grip with another chick at all.

***

"Yeah...so...um...I saw the way you were looking at ole' girl back at the mall," Marissa said with a smirk. "You feelin' her."

Grip and Marissa were chilling on the rooftop of her apartment when she stated the obvious. Although they weren't technically official, she was the only girl he took seriously and vice versa. They were platonic friends before anything else, which only solidified their bond. He'd met her back when he first moved to Georgia after his moms passed.

"Man, if you don't get on somewhere. Wasn't nobody checkin' for that damn girl. Chill."

"Whatever. I saw it all over your face," Marissa insisted. "The way you lit up when you—"

"Aight, you exaggerating now. Fall back, M," Grip laughed. It was relatively warm outside, and the fresh air felt good. Grip savored the moments away from his uncle and all the chaos.

"So...we gon' fuck her?" Marissa asked with a sly smile. On several occasions, they'd indulged in threesomes since Marissa loved pretty women too.

"Man, gon' with that shit. That's my uncle's girl."

Marissa became wide-eyed, like she just discovered something. "Damn, B. You gon' end up in a messy one—"

"Me and Kirby just cool. We know each other from high school. I told you it ain't even like that."

Marissa stared at him sideways. She didn't believe Grip for a second. She saw it in his eyes. He could feed her that bullshit all he wanted, but she knew him better than he knew himself sometimes. With a half smirk, she mumbled, "*Yet.*"

"Stop worryin' about Kirby and start worryin' about this dick." Grip tugged on her shirt, pulling her closer. Marissa wasted no time unbuttoning his jeans.

"Is that what you want me to do, Grip?" she asked, gazing into his eyes.

After pulling out his thick, rock hard dick, she stroked him gently in her hand. They were seated on a beach chair overlooking the entire Atlanta. All alone on the rooftop, they were free to do whatever they pleased.

Grip watched as she dipped her head low and took all 9 inches in her mouth. Marissa was the homie, but she sucked his dick like she was wifey. Maybe that's what she wanted in the end. Either way, he appreciated the satisfaction.

Grip was close to nutting when his iPhone buzzed. It was his uncle letting him know they had business they needed to handle. *Shit. What this mothafucka want now?* His uncle had the worst fucking timing.

"Is everything cool?" Marissa asked.

"We gon' have to come back to this. I gotta slide real quick."

Marissa rolled her eyes. "You *would* have to go before you take care of me."

"What can I say? Duty calls."

***

"There go that young nigga right there," Castle acknowledged. Ashing his Cohiba cigar, he removed his Gucci frames to study the teenage boy he'd caught in his daughter's bed. Seated in the Escalade with him was Grip and two of his shooters.

It didn't take much to find out where Tony lived and worked. Unfortunately, Tony didn't know that Castle wasn't done with him yet. He had just clocked out from an 8-hour shift at the pizza restaurant he worked at. He was a decent kid, but Castle didn't give a damn. The mothafucka needed to be taught a lesson.

Back in 2000, Castle and his brother Benny had beef with some rival competition. Femi had recently given birth to their first child—a little boy they named Knight who was two months old at the time. They'd just left a restaurant and were stationary at a red light when a black van pulled alongside them. Before Castle realized what was happening, they lit up his whip with AK-12s before peeling off in haste. Castle took four shots to his torso, and his son was murdered in cold blood. Femi and Castle never told Princess that story, and she never found out she'd had an older brother. That was mainly the reason behind her father's over-protectiveness— though he was known to go overboard with a lot of shit.

Tony barely had a chance to hit the locks on his old school Chevy before he was snatched up from behind and tossed in their truck. Seated in the backseat with a look of vengeance was Castle. Resting in his lap was a shiny Beretta with a suppressor screwed on the end.

Tony practically pissed himself when he saw the gun.

"Relax. Let's take a lil' ride. I wanna holla at you 'bout somethin'."

Tony tried his best to ease back in his seat. Something didn't feel right, but he still did as he was told. Fifteen minutes later, he regretted the decision to not flee sooner. *This nigga on some other shit.* Swallowing the large lump that formed in his throat, Tony watched the Escalade pull into an empty parking garage at the airport.

Castle played it off like he wanted to talk, when in all actuality he just wanted to get the kid alone where no witnesses would be present.

"W—wait. What is this shit? Wh—why am I here?" Tony stuttered. He nervously looked from Grip to Castle. He knew the reason he was there, but he still demanded answers.

Castle and his boys hopped out the truck. They had no qualms about terrorizing a minor. They'd all done worse shit in their corrupted lives.

"Get his pussy ass out," Castle ordered. He didn't have all day to play games and answer questions. He was a man of action, and a firm believer of consequences.

Tony actually had the nerve to try to lock himself inside. The poor boy was terrified. When he woke up that day nothing could've prepared him for being kidnapped and possibly killed by his girlfriend's father. Unfortunately, Princess failed to mention that her dad was a ruthless kingpin.

Grip snatched the kid out the truck and tossed him onto the concrete. He couldn't believe Castle made him cut his date short. He could've been getting some sloppy top, but instead he had to deal with this shit. He really wasn't feeling what they planned on doing, but there was no arguing with a nigga like his uncle. Castle had his own set of codes. His men simply followed suit; they never disputed him in any of his decision-making—no matter how unethical.

"C'mon man. Don't do this shit. I ain't mean no disrespect!" Tony pled. He was only seventeen. He wasn't ready to die. There were still so many things he hadn't experienced; so many places he hadn't seen.

The look on Castle's face showed he didn't give a fuck. When his hand went to his Beretta, Tony's life flashed before his eyes. Castle loved to use ruthless tactics to ensure power and control.

"Please, man—I swear to God me and Princess never fucked."

Upon hearing his daughter's name, Castle rushed the kid and yoked him up. Handling him like the hoe ass nigga he was, Castle slammed Tony against the truck and mushed him. "You talk too damn much, mufucka! Open yo' mouth!" Castle pressed the gun against his face.

"Hell naw—"

"I SAID OPEN YO' FUCKIN' MOUTH!" Castle hollered. "Bitch nigga, open up or I'm puttin' a hole through yo' mufuckin' head!"

When Tony didn't move fast enough, Castle shoved the barrel in his grill, busting his lip in the process. Blood leaked onto the cold, steel. Castle was unforgiving in his assault. Slowly moving the gun back and forth, he simulated oral sex. The shit was beyond embarrassing for Tony.

"Yeah...you wanna young bitch to suck on that lil' dick, huh?" Castle asked. "That's what you want?"

Tony's response came out muffled. Snot oozed from his nostrils as he cried like a baby. He just knew he was going to die that day. And the most fucked up thing about it was that he and Princess never actually had sex. They fondled around from time to time, but she never let him stick it in.

Grip, unable to watch the debasing act, turned his head away. He didn't always agree with the fucked up shit his uncle did, but he'd never actually tried to put a stop to it either. Yet as he stood there, listening to the kid cower in fear, he couldn't help but think that Castle had gone too far this time.

"Princess ain't that bitch though, homie. You hear me?"

Tony nodded his head sheepishly.

"Pussy nigga, I said do you hear me?" Castle repeated. He slapped Tony a few times in order to shake him up. When that didn't satisfy him, Castle pressed the barrel of the gun against his cheek. "Answer me."

"Yeah, I hear you, man. I got it."

"Nah, I don't think you got it." Still unconvinced, Castle bashed him in his broken nose with the butt of the gun. He didn't give a damn that the kid was still wearing a splint. In silence, everyone watched as Castle brutally pistol-whipped his daughter's boyfriend. By the time, he had finally tired himself out Tony was lying helplessly on the ground in a puddle of his own blood. His face, now barely recognizable, was a bloody distorted mess.

Grip felt bad as he watched Tony struggle to stand. The poor kid could barely move. Castle had really done a number on him. His bottom lip was split wide open, his nose was twisted an awkward angle, and his left eye had swollen completely shut. Blood leaked from every orifice. Castle had almost killed him. There was no doubt that he'd need reconstructive surgery after today.

Without remorse, Castle turned him over with his foot and placed the dirty sole of his Timberland on top of Tony's cheek. He was barely conscious as he looked up at Castle with one blood-filled eye. Tony knew it was the end when he cocked the gun and aimed at his head—

"Unc! Damn, man. Don't you think he's had enough," Grip finally spoke up. "I think he gets the fuckin' picture, yo."

If looks could kill, Castle would've murdered him a dozen times over. He didn't appreciate being challenged—especially in front of others. Nevertheless, he did somewhat agree. *I'll holla at his ass later 'bout that shit though*, Castle told himself.

"Since my nephew's feelin' humble right now, I guess today's ya lucky day," he said. "But if I catch ya ass near my daughter again, I won't hesitate to squeeze. Ya dig?"

Castle tucked his gun away and climbed inside the truck. His entourage followed suit, leaving Tony to bleed out alone. He didn't try to move again until the Escalade had finally pulled off. Thanks to Grip, he was still breathing.

Coughing and choking on blood, Tony struggled to stand. His entire face was on fire, as if he'd been injected with Lidocaine. After gaining his footing, he limped towards the exit. Anger manifested in his heart with each step he took. Castle would pay for the fucked up shit he did. By the time Tony finished with him, Castle would wish he had pulled the trigger.

Payback was a mothafucka.

12

Knock!

Knock!

Knock!

Light raps followed the doorbell ringing. Padding barefoot to the front entrance of her grand Virginia Highlands home, Femi wondered who would pop up unexpectedly. Monica was out of town on business so she knew it wasn't her.

Securing the robe around her bosom, Femi slowly opened the front door. She looked surprised to see Aviance standing there with a smug expression on his handsome face. He looked dapper that day in a Helmut tee, skinny jeans, and black high-top Prada sneakers. His cut was fresh, and he smelled of Giorgio Armani. As usual, his swag was on a thousand. Femi could take one look at Aviance and tell he emulated Castle. He was like a father figure to Aviance after taking him under his wing at 13. Femi watched as he quickly grew from a boy into a fine ass young man.

"Hey...what are you doing here?" she asked. "Castle left a few hours ago." Femi had no idea that he'd gone off to terrorize their daughter's boyfriend.

Licking his lips, Aviance took a step forward. Without warning, he tugged on her sash, releasing her robe. Femi didn't bother putting up a fight as he took in the mouthwatering sight of her naked chocolate body. Castle had paid for her breast lift 2 years ago, and those motherfuckers were sitting just right. His dick instantly sprang to life.

"You know damn well I ain't come here for Castle..." Aviance handed her the red rose he'd been hiding behind his back.

A smile slowly blossomed on Femi's pouty lips. After accepting the flower, she politely stepped to the side allowing him entrance.

Aviance let himself in and quietly closed the door behind him. He'd been fantasizing about swimming in her pussy since he got back in the A. Femi seductively bit her bottom lip in anticipation. There wasn't a single person alive who knew about their affair. They'd been fucking around for nearly a year with no intentions of ever stopping.

Aviance had been feeling Femi since the day he first laid eyes on her. Castle was his nigga and all, but his attraction to Femi was far greater than his loyalty to his boss. Besides, Castle couldn't fully commit to taking care of her needs like Aviance could. He was too busy chasing hoes in the street.

She'd gotten close to Aviance after noticing the way he looked at her whenever her husband wasn't watching. It was the same way Castle used to look at her back in the day. Castle would bury them if he ever found out the truth, but it was a risk she was willing to take.

"Is Princess home?" Aviance asked in a low tone.

Femi shook her head. "She's with her friends."

Aviance responded by pulling Femi close and kissing her roughly. He could no longer wait, or waste time with idle convo. He wanted her badly. "I been thinkin' 'bout you nonstop," he whispered.

"Yeah, yeah. Whatever. Sure you have."

"Swear to God."

"You hardly ever reach out."

"I never be knowin' when you're with him."

Femi curled her mouth up. Aviance had good game.

It seemed like every time McKenzie got under his skin he went running to Femi. She was his forbidden fruit, and he was her comfort zone. They both knew what they were doing was wrong, but neither wanted to put a stop to it. Something about sneaking around excited them.

Peeling the robe from her soft skin, Aviance watched as the silk material melted around her ankles.

"We may have an hour or two," Femi breathed. She could feel his erection pressing against her midsection and it turned her on.

"Shit, that's all a nigga needs."

13

Aviance placed a delicate trail of kisses along Femi's shoulder. They'd just finished fucking in the guest bedroom upstairs. Draped in sweaty sheets, they spooned together like an old married couple.

"Can I ask you a question?" his breath tickled the nape of Femi's neck, causing her nipples to harden.

"What's up?"

"When you gon' leave that nigga alone and be with me?"

"You know it's not that easy, Aviance. We've had this talk plenty of times—"

"You don't think I can take care of you?"

"That's not the point, bay."

"I get tired of sneakin' the fuck around like we kids, Femi. Got me feelin' like the side nigga or some shit."

"Would you rather we stopped?"

"That ain't what the fuck I want, Femi. I want you. I've always wanted yo' ass. But instead I gotta watch you play second fiddle to these hoes Castle be chasin'. I'd never do you like that."

"You got hoes too," Femi reminded him.

"Man, I'd let all them bitches go for you. You mean that much to a nigga."

"How sweet."

"I'm serious, Femi."

"I need time, Aviance. I can't just up and leave my husband. I have a family."

"So I'm not your family?"

"You know what I'm saying."

Aviance paused for a second. He thought about pressing the issue, but he knew that would only bring about an argument. He decided to change the subject. "Do you think I been wastin' my time with Castle all these years?"

Femi craned her head to look at him like he was crazy. "What?" she laughed. "Boy, what are you talking about? You must be letting that young, Philly hoe get in your head. You should've never ran your mouth to her about the business." Femi knew Aviance wasn't smart enough to come up with that alone. Someone had to have been in his ear.

Aviance playfully bit her arm. "Come on now, chill with the name callin'. And I wouldn't quite say I let her get in my head. She just brought up a valid point last time we were together. I mean, I been bustin' my ass for Castle since I was a kid...and for what?"

"What do you mean for what? You make good money, don't you? What's there to complain about?"

Aviance wanted to say more, but he remembered that Femi was Castle's wife. Of course, she was going to defend her husband. Her loyalty was obviously with him. *She'll never get it*, he told himself.

"What are you hinting at, Aviance?"

"Nothing. Forget I even mentioned it."

Pulling the sheets off his body, he slowly climbed out the bed and prepared to dress.

"You're leaving so soon?" Femi asked, disappointed. "The house will be empty for another hour or so—"

Aviance avoided eye contact. "Yeah, I gotta couple moves I need to make."

Femi resisted the urge to pout. She knew he was in his feelings about something, but she wouldn't hound him. "Well, when am I gonna see you again?"

Aviance was just about to respond, but the sound of movement from behind stopped him.

"WHAT THE FUCK?!"

Femi and Aviance both turned their attention to the person standing in the doorway. Their worst nightmare had just come to life...

14

"Yo," Castle answered his phone in a muffled voice. It was 8 in the damn morning and Kirby was blowing him up like she was crazy.

"Where are you? You haven't been here in days. I miss you. I'm sorry about everything that happened between us. I really just want you to come home."

Luckily, the chick lying beside Castle was asleep and couldn't hear how desperate Kirby sounded. She was supposed to be mad at him for cheating, but now she just wanted him back. She'd become so needy and dependent that self-respect no longer existed. Castle should've been apologizing to her, but as usual Kirby gave in first.

"You don't miss a nigga, for real," Castle challenged. He knew she did, but he got a kick out of her emptiness. Whenever he wasn't in the picture, his bitches grew hopeless and restless. They either missed the money, the dick, the attention, or all three.

"I promise I do," Kirby insisted. "I don't wanna fight with you. I just want you to come home. I don't like sleeping alone, bay..."

Castle paused as he thought about it. "You gon' gimme some of dat wet mouth when

I come back?" he asked, as if he deserved his dick sucked.

"Yes," Kirby purred.

All of a sudden, Castle's female friend stirred awake. "Who are you talkin' to?" Trina grumbled.

"Who is *that*?" Kirby demanded to know. "You're with a bitch, aren't you?"

"Look, I'mma hit you back later, aight."

"Castle—"

Click.

Kirby pulled the phone away from her face and stared at it. *That motherfucker!* "I got something for his ass though!"

Jumping out the bed, she quickly threw on some clothes and pulled her hair up in a ponytail. She knew where the Nudie bitch lived, and she planned on popping up unannounced to get her man back.

"Where are you going?" Her mother, Leah called out from her bedroom.

Fully dressed, Kirby stopped in her doorway. "Out really fast. I'll be back though."

Leah sighed in frustration. Her illness had definitely taken its toll. She was weak and tired of seeing her daughter put up with a nigga who wasn't shit. "I know you ain't going to chase down that grown ass man."

"Ma, please," Kirby said with an attitude. She hardly ever spent any time with her because she was always so wrapped up in Castle. Leah's last days were approaching, but all Kirby seemed to care about was running after him.

"Kirby, let it be," she said weakly. "Nothing you do will make him change. I told you a long time ago, like my grandma told me 'never fall for a dog who has eyes for every bitch'," she snorted. "You let that slick-talkin' bastard move us down here where we don't have any friends or family—"

"Ma, we barely had any friends or family in Philly. Kaleb is in prison—"

"We had each other...minus all the bullshit," Leah said. "That was enough for me."

"Castle paid all your medical expenses, ma. Don't forget that. He tried to pay for your treatment too but—"

"I've already accepted my fate, Kirby. It's time you have too..."

Kirby looked down at her feet, unable to meet her mom's gaze. She became sad every time her mother talked about dying. It was so much easier to just avoid the topic altogether. It made Kirby feel like the day would never come. What would she do without her mom? Who would she have in her corner?

Kirby never knew if Castle was coming or going. Leah was her rock. How would she function without her?

"I don't wanna talk about this," Kirby told her. "Like I said, I'll be back."

Before Leah could oppose, Kirby was gone.

***

"Why you sittin' over there lookin' anxious? Like ya piss test came back positive or some shit? You look more nervous than a nigga in court with three strikes."

Grip and Aviance were on their way to meet with the Mexicans when he noticed his boy's demeanor. Aviance was steadily fidgeting and biting his nails. Something was definitely up.

"Nothin'. I'm good, man. I'm all good."

"You sure?" Grip asked. He knew Aviance better than he thought he did. He could tell when something was up.

Aviance blew out air and ran a hand through his short, curly Afro. His nerves were understandably on edge. He thought about telling Grip that Femi's daughter had caught them together, but he decided it was best not to. That would just be one more person who knew about their affair. Instead, he decided to voice his second concern.

"Man, McKenzie been houndin' me about doin' some crazy ass shit. That's why I ain't been fuckin' with her lately."

"Like what?"

Aviance cut his eyes at Grip. He was skeptical about mentioning it, but he figured he'd keep it real. "I almost feel fucked up tellin' you this shit...but McKenzie thinks I should rob Castle and start my own business. She says I've been still for too long."

Grip remained quiet because lately he hadn't been fucking with his uncle anyway. Castle was fam and all, but the mothafucka was out of control and drunk off power. Aviance assumed Grip's silence meant he felt some type of way. At the end of the day, Castle was his family.

"But I'm not though," Aviance quickly added.

"Is that why you actin' jumpy and shit?" Grip suddenly wondered if he could trust Aviance himself.

"I'm good," Aviance reassured him. "Never mind what I mentioned. Forget I even said the shit."

"Aight then. Well, get it together, bruh. We almost here."

Grip did not want Aviance coming off as suspicious to the Migos. Castle needed his connects just as badly as the fiends needed the dope. The Mexicans smuggled in bricks and delivered to the Mafia. It was Aviance and Grip's job to meet them at the drop off point and transport the drugs to the trap houses.

"I told you I'm straight." There was slight annoyance in Aviance's tone. He had a lot on his mind. All Princess had to do was tell her father what she saw, and he was a dead man. Shit couldn't have been any worse for him.

***

Kirby, hell-bent on making a scene, hopped out the Uber car and slammed the door. She was tired of being disrespected and cheated on.

Luna lived in the *Mezzo* luxury apartments on Peachtree Rd., not too far from where she stayed. It didn't take much to track her down after posting her nude photo. When Kirby finally found the bitch's Instagram page, she saw a bunch of pictures with her and Castle. A few had even been snapped while he lay sleeping beside her. The worst part was that most of the photos were recently dated. Castle had been fucking with Luna while they were still together.

Unfortunately, both of them were in for a rude awakening that morning. Kirby located Luna's unit number from the call box downstairs and promptly made her way to the elevators. She impatiently rode it up to the 9th floor. It felt like she couldn't get off fast enough.

As soon as Kirby reached her door, she pounded with a closed fist. "Open the door! I know your ass is in there!"

BOOM!

BOOM!

BOOM!

Kirby slammed her fist against the wooden surface in angst. She would've kicked the door off the hinges if she could.

"Open the door!" Kirby yelled. She didn't give a damn about the neighbors hearing her at 9 something in the morning. She was just about to holler a string of obscenities when she heard movement beyond the door.

After unlocking her bolt, Luna cracked the door open just a little. She was a thick redbone with slanted eyes and pouty lips. Her dark brown hair was cut in a Chinese bob. The 23-year old was cute, definitely Castle's type. That made Kirby even angrier.

"Are you fucking crazy?" Luna snapped. She was getting a good night's sleep before Kirby showed up on one. She also woke up her son. "Why are you banging on my damn door this early like you crazy?"

Kirby would've reached through the door and slapped her had it not been for the infant she was holding. Her eyes lingered on the adorable chocolate little boy. He looked a lot like...

Luna quickly interrupted Kirby's thoughts. "Yo' ass *must* have the wrong address."

"I doubt that. Is Castle inside? And don't play stupid. I saw the pics all over your IG page. I know ya'll fucking around."

Luna scoffed and shook her head in pity. "Little girl, I know you ain't pop up at my house for that sorry ass nigga. Look boo, he ain't here. Ain't been in months."

"Well, why are you sending him naked pics?"

"'Cuz that's the only way to gage that trifling ass nigga. I have to *persuade* him just to come the fuck around to take care of his responsibilities. Speaking of which, when you see that sorry mothafucka, let him know his son needs diapers."

Kirby's mouth fell open. She couldn't believe what she was hearing. It felt like she'd just been gut punched. "What are you talking about? Castle does not have a son!"

Luna laughed at Kirby's lack of knowledge. Apparently, she didn't know her man as well as she thought she did. "Girl, stop it. I saw the expression on your face when you looked at CJ. You know as well as I do that this is his son."

Kirby shook her head. She just couldn't accept the truth because it hurt so badly. "That's bullshit. Castle told me he didn't have any kids—"

Luna broke out laughing even harder at Kirby's ignorance. When she first popped up at her door, Luna wanted to choke her...now she just felt sorry for Kirby. "Castle is a liar and a manipulator! Is that what he told you?" she asked. "That mothafucka ain't shit. I swear he ain't. But I guess that's to be expected of him. You ain't the only one though so don't feel too bad. He done fed me a shitload of lies too, girl. Hell, last summer he promised we'd get married after finding out I was pregnant."

Kirby didn't know what to say. She didn't want to look like a fool even though she felt like a fool. And she surely didn't want Luna to know she was getting to her. "I still think you full of shit. Castle ain't got no kids."

Luna just shook her head. "Girl, Castle has a son, a 16-year old daughter, *and* a wife! Did you know all that?"

It almost felt like a rug had been snatched from underneath her. Kirby wanted to scream 'lies', but she had a feeling there was truth to Luna's accusations.

Kirby came looking for a confrontation, but she got way more than what she bargained for. *Castle was married with two kids*? How could he lie to her for so long?

"How did you meet Castle?" Kirby asked.

"I was dancing at Magic City at the time. He walked up on me and told me he wanted to eat my pussy and he ain't give a fuck what it smelled like. Those were his words exactly."

Kirby frowned. That sounded like some shit Castle would say. He loved eating pussy more than fucking.

"Do you wanna come inside?" Luna offered. Her tone momentarily softened after seeing how upset Kirby was. It wasn't too long ago when she found out the truth for herself. Castle had strung her along for over year and a half. She wished like hell someone would've told her the facts before she got knocked up. But CJ was there, and she wouldn't have traded him for anything in the world.

Kirby slowly nodded her head. She could barely formulate a sentence; her mind was all over the place.

Unlocking the door, Luna cracked it open and stepped to the side. She had a shitload of dirt she needed to catch Kirby up on. After today, she would never look at her man the same.

15

It was a quarter after noon when Castle finally called Kirby. She was back at home, still astounded by all that Luna had told her. Kirby tried watching television to take her mind off it, but she could hardly focus. Soon the TV was watching her.

Kirby stared at the name displayed on her screen. She almost didn't want to speak to his lying ass, but she deserved answers. "Hello?"

Castle sucked his teeth. "Damn. Why a nigga gotta get that dry ass greetin'? Yo' ass must be over there mad still. Ma, let that shit go. I thought you missed me...or were you flexin'?"

"I did..." Kirby answered through tight lips. "But that was before I caught you laid up with some bitch."

"Fuck is you talkin' 'bout? I ain't been fuckin' with nobody. A nigga been to himself, stayin' out the way of bitch ass niggas. I was not laid up with no hoes—"

"Bullshit. I heard her voice in the background."

"That don't mean I was with a fuckin' bitch. Shit, I been stayin' at my grandma's to blow some steam."

"Your grandma's?" Kirby asked skeptically. She was insulted by how stupid Castle thought she was. "You really expect me to believe that? Your grandma just happens to sound like she's in her twenties? Really?"

Castle wasn't feeling the sarcasm in her tone. "Look, we gon' go back and forth about the shit, or you gon' let me make up lost time? I missed yo' lil' ass."

Kirby pulled the phone away from her face and sighed. She didn't want shit to do with him...but for some reason she couldn't bring herself to say it. Kirby loved Castle far too much to just walk away. He'd rescued her from poverty and took care of her and her mom. What would she do without him in her life? Where would she go?

"How?" Kirby simply asked. "How are you gonna make it up to me?"

"I'mma swing by later on. We can go on a date or some shit."

Kirby's eyes instantly lit up at the sound of that. It wasn't often that they enjoyed recreational couple's activities. Castle stayed in the streets so much. Usually, his definition of a date was Netflix and take-out, and he almost always fell asleep on whatever movie she decided on. Either way, Kirby enjoyed the quality time they shared. Those occasions were a rarity.

"Really?"

"Yeah. Be ready and downstairs by nine, aight?"

"Okay. I will be," Kirby said excitedly. Just like that all of her anger towards him vanished.

"Anyway, what'cho ass been doin' these last few days?"

"Nothing much, really. McKenzie's in town, and the other day I went over Grip's to re-twist his dreads."

Castle grimaced. "Ya'll mufuckas a lil' too chummy."

"You know it's not like that. Since McKenzie be fucking with Aviance we just all got cool. Plus me and him went to high school together."

Castle rubbed his goatee as he listened. He found that mighty funny, because when he asked Grip once if he knew Kirby from Philly he said no. Why would the nigga lie?

"I don't want you hangin' with them niggas like that."

"But McKenzie is Aviance's girl," she argued.

"Are you Aviance's bitch?"

"No."

"Aight then. Shut the fuck up sometimes. Listen to what I tell yo' ass. I don't want you kickin' it heavy with them."

"Alright," Kirby mumbled, knowing damn well she still was going to.

Before Castle disconnected the call, he asked, "You love me, baby girl?"

Kirby didn't miss a beat. "Yes, baby. I do. You know I do."

"How much?"

"A whole lot. More than is measurable."

"I'mma see you later on, lil' lady."

After ending the call, Kirby raced to her walk-in closet and searched for the sexiest red dress she could find.

Meanwhile, Castle's 21-year old piece, Trina stared daggers at him from her bathroom's doorway. "I see you waited good until I went to pee to call up yo' bitch. I heard everything. You think you fucking slick, Castle, but you not," she sassed. "You promised you were gonna spend the day with me. I just heard you making plans with someone else."

"Stop eavesdropping and you won't hear shit you ain't 'posed to." Castle was never the type to admit his wrongs. After all, the women took him back, regardless, no matter how fucked up he treated them.

"What does that mean? Are you gonna spend the day with me or not?" she whined.

Castle placed his phone on the nightstand beside the bed. "You know what? That's what yo' problem is right there. You talk too fuckin' much sometimes, Trina. Miss me with all the questions. Matter fact, get over here and suck this dick."

Since Castle paid all her bills including the car note and rent for the 3-bedroom apartment, she willingly did as told. Pleased with her submissiveness, he watched her grab his pole and kiss the tip. Pre-cum leaked onto her small hand; he was so big that she could only fit three-quarters in her mouth.

"*Mmm.* Does your wife suck it like this, baby?"

Castle suddenly snatched her up by her weave. "Don't be cute, bitch. And don't think I forgot that shit you did. Next time you call my wife, I'm fucking you up!" Castle forced her mouth back onto his dick before firing up a blunt. Trina's head continued to bob up and down in his lap like he hadn't said shit wrong. She was crazy about the motherfucker. "That pussy wasn't feelin' as tight as it usually do," he told her. "I hope you ain't givin' my shit to no other niggas when I ain't here."

"I'm not. I swear."

Castle grabbed a fistful of her hair. "For yo' sake, you better be tellin' the God's honest truth," he threatened. "'Cuz if I find out yo' ass is fuckin' somebody else, I'mma kill you and that nigga."

***

As promised, Castle arrived at Kirby's residence a little after 9 p.m. She was already waiting downstairs in the lobby when he pulled up in a white Cadillac Escalade stretch limousine. *Typical.* He loved showing out. Castle would do just about anything to garner attention.

Sashaying towards the flashy limo, Kirby looked beautiful in a red off-the-shoulder bandage dress. She wasn't the curviest girl but she filled it out well. It also made her booty look nice and plump.

"Hey, baby. I missed you," she sang, climbing in. Kirby pecked his lips before raining kisses all over his face. "You did this for me?" The luxury limo boasted a full bar, TV, and colorful strobe lights.

Castle hugged Kirby and squeezed her ass. "Of course, bay. The best for the best. You look good. Smell good too." Despite the way he treated her, Castle cherished her young, loyal ass. He had no intentions whatsoever of letting her go anytime soon. "Here, I got you somethin'." Castle passed her the Nordstrom's bag. Inside was a brand new Louis Vuitton purse.

Kirby anxiously pulled it out and admired it. "Thank you, baby! Oh my God. I love it!"

Castle cleaned up nicely that evening. He had a fresh line up and was covered in a black Burberry suit with crocodile Tom Ford loafers. He looked so professional and well put together that no one would ever assume he sold drugs for a living.

After embracing her man, Kirby took a seat beside him. She saw that he'd already started drinking and snorting lines.

Kirby had never touched the drugs even though she was exposed to it on a daily basis. On one occasion, she expressed an interest in trying it, and Castle slapped the shit out of her. He didn't want her turned out and pinching off his work. He kept a few kilos and cash at each woman's home in case he ever needed to make a quick getaway.

"So...where we going?"

"Houston's. I gotta taste for some steak and some pussy for dessert." Castle placed his hand on Kirby's thigh and squeezed it gently.

She thought about asking where he really was the last few days, but she knew she wouldn't get the truth. She never did.

Kirby tried her best to push her worries to the back of her mind and enjoy the ride. But it was harder to do so than she imagined. Kirby couldn't stop replaying everything Luna had told her. *Do I really know this nigga as well as I think I do?*

"What's up? You look bothered by somethin'," Castle said. "You good?"

Kirby nervously twiddled her thumbs while chewing her bottom lip. She deserved to know the truth, but a part of her was scared to. It would change everything. What she and Castle had wasn't perfect, but in her feeble mind it was the next best thing.

"Yeah...I'm good..." she lied.

All of a sudden, CJ's face popped up in her head. He had Castle's eyes.

"You know what? Actually...I'm not good," Kirby told him. "I went to see your lil' girlfriend, Luna. She told me everything. About you having a son...about you being married. Is it true, Castle?"

Silence was the response she received. Instead of replying, he sat there annoyed. He was tired of her playing investigator. Why couldn't she sit the fuck still and cooperate like all the others. She just had to do the most.

"Don't get quiet now. Say something," Kirby insisted.

"Fuck that. Who the fuck told you to talk to dat bitch?"

"No one. I sought her out after seeing y'all pictures all over Instagram—"

"I told yo' ass to delete that shit. That's yo' fucking problem. You hardheaded. You do too damn much."

"Don't flip this on me, Castle. Is it true or not? Are you married?"

"...Yeah...but we in the middle of tryin' to file for a divorce," he lied.

"Why didn't you tell me?"

"'Cuz it ain't important. You my bitch now. The past don't matter, bay."

"Well, what do you mean 'trying'? Why haven't you already done it?"

"Divorces are expensive."

"So is this limo...and your suit...and my condo..."

"Kirby, don't get on my nerves today, man," he said, calmly. "Stop fuckin' diggin'. I'm tryin' to have a good night."

"How the hell can I enjoy myself with you knowing this?" Kirby cried. "You lied to me. You told me you didn't have kids but I saw your son today—"

"That ain't my fuckin' kid. I don't know who else done ran up in that hoe," Castle argued. "Why the fuck is you lettin' some bitch you don't know fuck up our night?"

"'Cuz you a fucking dog ass liar! What else don't I know? I fucking hate yo' ass—"

Castle slapped the shit out of Kirby. "*You hate me*? After everything I've done for yo' lil' ungrateful ass? I told you dat bitch was lyin'! You gon' take her word over mine?!"

Kirby grabbed her stinging cheek. She didn't expect him to react so harsh.

"You hate me?" he asked again. "That's how you really fuckin' feel?" Castle straightened up his suit and the collar to his dress shirt. He was tipsy and high on coke, so his reasoning was a little off. "Then get the fuck out my limo."

"What?"

"Bitch, you heard me." Castle reached over and banged on the partition. "Aye, pull this mufucka over real quick!" he demanded.

They were already on Lenox Rd. when Castle decided to ditch Kirby. He could enjoy a well-done steak on his own for all he gave a fuck.

The driver slowly brought the limo to a stop on the side of the street. Kirby couldn't believe he actually wanted her to get out.

"Fuck you sittin' there for? You dismissed. Get the fuck on."

"Castle? Really? You fucking serious?" Kirby was in disbelief.

"Since you hate my black ass so much ain't no sense in sharing space. Get the fuck out."

Kirby knew how mad he was, but she was still defiant. "I am not about to get out."

"I SAID GET THE FUCK OUT! 'Fore I put yo' ass out!" Castle hollered. He kicked the shit out of her leg to make her move faster.

They tussled a little before she was successfully thrown out on her ass. As soon as she hit the ground, the limo quickly sped off in haste, leaving her stranded. *Why the hell am I being punished when he's the one who fucked up?*

Kirby felt ridiculous, as she stood alone on the curb. Trails of mascara ran down her cheeks; she was livid. "How am I gonna get home?" In the heat of the moment, she'd left her purse and phone in the limo. Things had quickly gone from bad to worse.

***

Grip was cruising through Buckhead when he noticed a familiar face wandering down the street. He was only on that side of town because one of his patnas had opened a new little hookah lounge. He didn't expect to see Kirby along the way. For a second, he thought his eyes were playing tricks on him.

"Is that...? Nah, can't be..."

Grip lowered the music on his Drake album, as if that would make him see better. After seeing that it was indeed Kirby, he pulled over to the side of the street. Grip made sure to keep the pace of his truck equal to her walking. He didn't give a fuck about the annoyed drivers behind him honking their horns.

"Aye, Kirby!" Grip yelled through his lowered window.

Finally, she stopped long enough to glance at his G-wagon. His presence was a Godsend. Kirby's feet were hurting, but she had no money for a taxi or bus. Luckily, Grip was on that side of town when he was.

"You don't look dressed for exercising. What the hell you doin' out here walkin'?. You need a ride?"

He didn't have to ask twice. Kirby quickly rounded the truck, and Grip politely reached over and opened the door. He couldn't wait to hear whatever explanation she had.

As soon as Kirby climbed in, Grip noticed the dark mark on her leg. There was also a faint bruise on her left cheek. "Fuck happened?"

"Me and Castle got into it," she said.

Grip easily put two and two together. "Damn." He wanted to choke the nigga until his eyes bulged. Grip wasn't feeling his uncle putting his hands on her.

Kirby put her seatbelt on and looked out the window to mask her embarrassment. She still couldn't believe Castle had actually kicked her out the limo. He was the one who'd been cheating and lying. Why was she being disciplined? Kirby didn't quite hate him, but he damn sure made it hard to love him at times.

"That's my people and all, but how you let dat nigga treat you like that?"

"I love him..."

"Love hurt like a mufucka then," he mumbled. "Nigga got you out here walkin' around, lookin' like you just got in a bar fight or some shit."

Tears filled Kirby's eyes. "It's complicated, Grip."

"Man, I guess..." Grip had a soft spot for Kirby. He hated to see her hurt. It pissed him off. He wanted to do something about it, but what could he do? Castle was his uncle and Kirby was his girl.

Since she'd tired herself out from all the excuses, Kirby decided to keep quiet. She was well aware of how foolish she looked, but the truth was she loved Castle. Apart of her felt like he was too good for her. She wasn't ready to walk away.

Grip was just about to hop on the interstate when he heard her stomach growl. "You hungry?" he asked.

"I'm starving," she admitted. "Me and Castle was supposed to go to Houston's but..." her voice trailed off. She didn't want to talk about the limo incident. "I hadn't eaten anything because I wanted to save my appetite for our date."

Grip allowed his inner-hater to surface when he sucked his teeth and said, "Man, that place overrated as hell anyway."

His comment made her smile.

"What'chu gotta taste for?"

"I guess I was craving steak."

"Cool. I know a dope spot over there on Piedmont. That shit bang. Grab my phone for me real quick. I got the OpenTable app. My password's 5544."

Kirby frowned after unlocking his iPhone and seeing Marissa as his screensaver. "You must really love this chick since you got her as your background."

Grip chuckled. "She did that shit. I just never got around to changin' it."

"So do you?" Kirby pressed.

"Do I what?"

"Love her?"

Grip tore his gaze away from the road to look at Kirby. "Why all these questions about Marissa?"

"It's no big deal. I just didn't know you had a girl."

"You with my uncle. Does it matter?"

"No," Kirby lied. "Why would it?"

"Exactly." After shutting Kirby down, Grip turned up the music to his Drake CD.

What if I pick you up from your house...

We should get out...

We haven't talked in a while....

We should roll to see where it goes...

I saw potential in you from the go...

You know that I did...

Fifteen minutes later, Grip pulled up to *Bone's Restaurant.* Valet ran towards them to park the tank. Before they stepped out, Grip gave Kirby a napkin to wipe her face. After a quick once over in the mirrored sun visor, she climbed out. Kirby was comfortable having dinner with Grip, but apart of her still wished her date with Castle had fell through. He'd moved her down to ATL to be closer to him, but they hardly ever did anything together.

Since *Bone's* was filled to capacity, Kirby and Grip sat at the bar where they were served bread and appetizers. They talked and caught up as they waited on the main entrees. Enjoying herself with him came so naturally. Grip's earthy charisma, and dry sense of humor were her favorite qualities about him. For a second, she'd almost forgotten about her fight with Castle.

For the main entrees, Grip and Kirby both settled on medium-rare steaks with macaroni, and greens. They had some of the best food she'd ever eaten, and she was glad she took him up on his offer.

They had just finished dessert when Kirby decided to ask a question that had been bugging her. "Why you never tell me Castle was married, Grip?"

The question caught him off guard. Up until then, he had no idea that Kirby knew about his aunt. He didn't bother defending his reasoning.

"I wanted to say somethin'...but to be real, it ain't my place...."

Surprisingly, Kirby took it in stride. "...I get it..." she said. "He's your uncle and you ain't wanna be in the middle."

Grip started to tell her that he was already in the middle. He had feelings for Kirby, but it was clear whom her heart belonged to. She knew the truth about Castle, and she still hadn't left the nigga. He doubted she ever would.

Subsequently following their dinner date, Grip suggested they go to *Uptown Comedy Corner*. He hoped it would put her in better spirits because he could tell she was still down about Castle. And as they say 'laughter was the best medicine'. He knew it wasn't the best idea to be out kicking it with Kirby. Atlanta was small and Castle was a well-known figure. But the truth was, he enjoyed her company too much to give a fuck.

Kirby hadn't laughed so hard in years. She was too busy distracted by her mother's illness, Kaleb's imprisonment, and her troubling relationship with Castle. It felt so good to just let go and have fun.

After the comedy show ended, Grip turned his phone on as they walked out together. He wouldn't tell Kirby he'd cut it off just to have some privacy with her. When his iPhone finally powered on, Castle was blowing him up.

Shit. What this nigga want now?

Had someone seen him and Kirby together and said something?

"Hold on real quick." Grip stepped off to the side to answer. "Yo', what up, unc'."

"Fuck you at? I need you down at the warehouse a.s.a.p."

Grip looked over at Kirby. He was playing with fire and he knew it.

"Is everything cool?"

"Just get ya ass down here." Castle hung up, and Grip was left wondering what was so pressing.

Shoving his phone in his back pocket, Grip walked over to Kirby.

She must've noticed something was up because she asked, "Is everything okay?"

"Gotta handle some business."

"Oh," she said flatly.

Grip didn't miss the disappointment in her tone. He wasn't the only one unhappy about cutting their evening short. He loved spending time with her. They were so compatible. It was as if they were already a couple. She felt familiar, like he'd known her forever.

"Ya boy just summoned me," Grip said unenthused.

Kirby looked nervous. "Who? Castle?"

"Yup."

"*Mmph.* What did he want?"

"Not sure yet."

Together Grip and Kirby climbed in his G-Wagon. The ride back to her Midtown apartment was quiet. There were so many things running through his mind. He wasn't supposed to be caking with his uncle's lady and shit, but Grip couldn't deny the palpable chemistry they shared.

After pulling in front of her residence, Grip parked and turned to face her. "How's your mom?"

"You should come in real quick and ask her yourself."

Grip knew he should've been hightailing it to the warehouse, but he figured he had a few extra minutes to spare. "Aight."

Together he and Kirby made their way inside and upstairs to her unit. Leah was in her bedroom watching re-runs of *Desperate Housewives*. She looked a little better that evening. She had her good days and her bad days. As soon as she saw Kirby and Grip appear in her doorway she smiled.

"Hello, Ms. Caldwell. How you feeling?" Grip walked over and gave her a gentle hug.

"Hanging in there," she said. "How 'bout you?"

"Can't complain."

"You been stayin' out of trouble?"

"Yes ma'am."

"He's lying," Kirby cut in.

They all shared a laugh since they knew it was true.

Leah loved seeing him and her daughter together. She always thought he was more fitting for her. Even though he was a little rough around the edges she could see that he had a good heart. As much as he tried to hide it, she could also see how strongly he felt about Kirby.

"Come by and visit more," Leah told him. "Don't be a stranger, you hear me."

"I'll do that," Grip promised.

After bidding each other farewell, Kirby walked him to the front door. "Thanks...for everything, Grip..."

"Whatever, punk. Just stay outta trouble."

"I'll try...but I can't make any promises..."

The two of them lingered at the door for a second. Neither was ready to say goodbye. All of a sudden, Grip took the impulsive initiative by pinning her against the door and kissing her. Instead of fighting it, Kirby wrapped her legs around his waist. Truth be told, she wanted him just as badly as he wanted her.

Her arms went around his neck as he showered her throat with fervent kisses. His grip on her tiny waist was firm. When he bit her shoulder she shivered in response. "Grip," she breathed. "Grip...wait...No...this ain't right..." Kirby said one thing but her body said another. In an attempt to be the bigger person, she slid down and tried to walk off, but he grabbed and yanked her against him.

Before she could protest, his tongue slid inside her mouth. Kirby's hand went to his chest, and his to her waist. She responded with such enthusiasm that he lifted her off her feet. Kirby wrapped her legs around his waist, like that was where he belonged. Her fingers slid up his t-shirt and across his six-pack before settling on his erection. She gave his 9-inches a gentle squeeze, savoring the thought of him being deep inside her.

Once again, Grip backed her against the door and that time she didn't protest. He lifted up her dress and was surprised to see that she wasn't wearing a bra. Grip hungrily took her small breast in his mouth and with a yearning need. Her nipples pebbled under his slippery tongue. She had him harder than a mothafucka—especially with the way she was bucking against him.

Grip's tongue moved to her cleavage before traveling upward. Kirby was in heaven. She loved how tender and passionate he was.

Grip made a trail of kisses up her chest to the side of her neck. She almost creamed in her panties when he sucked on her lobe and blew in her ear. Her name left his lips in a desperate and hoarse whisper. He could no longer contain himself.

"I want'cho mufuckin ass. And I don't mean just fuckin'. I want all of you, Kirby..."

She quickly removed his rubber band so that she could run her fingers through his dreads. "Take me, baby," she moaned.

Grip would have if it weren't for Castle blowing him up at that very moment. He wanted to know where the fuck his nephew was.

"Shit," Grip groaned in frustration. Kirby could see the annoyance in his expression. "I don't want to, but I gotta roll..."

Kirby slid down from his body and hastily got decent. She felt a little embarrassed for having allowed things to go as far as they did. Castle would kill them if he ever found out.

Grip opened the door. "I'mma get up with you later, aight."

After leaving Kirby with her panties wet, he headed straight to the warehouse to meet Castle. On the short ride there, he thought about what his uncle might want to talk about. It was a quarter after 1 a.m. when he swaggered inside. He expected to find Castle alone, but was surprised to see the whole gang in attendance when he arrived.

"About fuckin' time. We been waitin' on you, mufucka."

Grip looked around at all the angry expressions. For a second, he thought he was about to be ambushed...then he noticed the two men standing in the center of their ring. Apparently, they were the core of the issue.

"Wassup?" Grip asked.

His boys, Anderson and Boomer stood opposite of each other as the gang surrounded them. If Grip didn't know any better he'd think they were about to be jumped in. Unfortunately, it was the exact opposite. Blood in. Blood out.

"Word got to me that these two mufuckas been stealin'. And there ain't shit worse than a mufuckin' thief in my book. So I'm exercisin' my right to discipline."

Grip looked confused. "*Discipline*?"

"Mufucka, did I stutter?" Castle snapped.

"Castle, don't do this shit, man. We like family," Anderson pled. He'd just had another baby, and the only reason he started pinching off was because he needed the extra cash.

Boomer just stood there in silence. He knew there wasn't shit he could say to change Castle's mind. A thief was a thief. Sadly, his greed would cost him his life.

A king who couldn't control his colony wasn't a king at all. If Castle didn't punish them, niggas would only continue to try him, and he couldn't have that.

"Lemme hold ya iron real quick," Castle told Grip. He held his hand out for the gun as everyone waited in suspense.

"Why?"

"Mufucka, you know I hate repeatin' myself..."

Grip sucked his teeth and blew out air, before giving him his piece.

"I need yours too, Aviance."

Aviance quickly did as he was told with no opposition whatsoever. For a nigga that was smashing out his wife, Aviance was the first one to kiss his ass. Grip was the only one who ever challenged Castle's authority.

After relieving both men of their burners, Castle cocked the guns one by one. Anderson and Boomer watched his every move with wide, fearful eyes. They just knew the end was near. Disloyalty could not go unpunished in the Mafia.

"I'll tell you what," Castle began. "Instead of killin' both you traitors, I'll give one of you mufuckas the opportunity to live..."

Grip frowned and turned his head away. Castle loved to reinforce his position by using brutal methods. Castle had known them since they were in middle school. But all that shit went out the window the second he found out they were stealing from him.

Castle surprised everyone when he handed the guns to Boomer and Anderson. "First nigga to put the other down, I'll let walk free."

"Man, I ain't tryin' to watch this bullshit," Grip said with an attitude. Anderson and Boomer were his friends. They were all just kicking it in the club together last weekend. Grip felt inhumane taking part.

The look Castle gave his nephew was murderous. "Bitch nigga, you gon' watch whatever the fuck I tell you to!" His loud, deep voice bounced off the walls in the warehouse. Castle wanted to make it clear that he ran shit. If Grip had a problem with it, then he could end up in a similar predicament as his boys.

Grip rolled his eyes but he didn't defy his uncle. Normally, he went against the grain yet now wasn't the time for bravado.

After putting Grip in his place, Castle turned back to face Anderson and Boomer.

They both looked afraid for what was to come next. There was never any telling with a deranged nigga like Castle. He was the King Joffrey of the drug game.

"Like I was sayin'... First nigga to put the other down, I'll let walk free."

Despite hearing the rules loud and clear, both men hesitated.

"What'chu mean?" Anderson asked.

"Nigga, am I speakin' a foreign fuckin' language?" Castle slapped him upside the head like he was stupid. "First one to pop the other gets let off the hook."

Anderson and Boomer stared at each other in bewilderment. Neither wanted to go through with it. They were homeboys; they practically grew up together while working for Castle.

"You want us to kill each other?" Anderson asked. He was the first to lower his gun. "Man, I can't do no shit like th—"

POP!

Boomer shot Anderson in the chest without a second thought. If their lives were on the line, then he would rather it be Anderson than him.

A sinister grin spread across Castle's lips. Justice was sweet.

Anderson's face contorted in pain as he grabbed his mid-section. He couldn't believe his boy had actually shot him. Dropping to his knees, he fell over sideways, landing on the cold concrete. He was losing blood incredibly fast, but no made an effort to call an ambulance. This was his end.

Castle was ruthless as he turned Anderson over with his crocodile loafers. Blood had splattered on his pants leg, but he didn't notice. "You feel that?" he cackled. "You feel that shit? That's the price of your nobility, pussy nigga."

Anderson coughed and choked on his own blood. With each second that passed he could slowly feel his life slipping away.

"That's some cold-hearted shit, man," Grip said. "You been knowin' the nigga since he was thirteen—"

"I ain't fuckin' cold-hearted. I'm logical," Castle told him. He slowly knelt down and picked up Anderson's gun. He then looked over at Boomer. The mere sight of him was disgusting. "Hell you still standin' here for? Get the fuck outta here 'fore I change my mind."

Boomer tossed the gun on the ground and turned to leave. His hands were still shaking. He'd never be able to sleep peacefully after that day.

The fellas parted so that he could leave, but Castle stopped him. "Aye, Boomer?"

"Yeah?"

POP!

Castle shot his big ass in the foot without a warning.

"*Ah, shit!*" Boomer screamed. He fell down onto the ground, moaning in pain while cradling his foot. He should've been lucky it wasn't his brain. Anderson's lifeless body lay several feet from where he was. It could've just as easily been him.

Castle broke out laughing at Boomer's misfortune. His simple ass didn't even see it coming. He should've run out that motherfucker.

Across the room, Grip shook his head in pity. His uncle had no chill. *I'm really startin' to hate this cocky nigga*, he thought. Between this, the incident with Tony, and what he'd done to Kirby, Grip didn't know how much longer he could deal with Castle.

"Get the fuck up and get'cho dumb ass outta here," he told Boomer. "Fat fuck."

Everyone watched as he struggled to stand. Blood leaked from his gaping open wound. If he didn't get to a hospital fast then he would bleed out, and Anderson's death would be in vain.

Grip made a move to help Boomer, but Castle quickly pointed his gun at him. "Ain't nobody ask you to play hero, mufucka. Back up. Let him help himself like he did with my yayo."

Boomer managed to stand on his own with little balance. He limped out of the room thankful his life was spared.

"Let that be a lesson to all you mufuckas," Castle said. "Now get the fuck outta here and back to the money. Meeting's adjourned."

16

"The other day Princess called me a pessimistic bitch. Can you believe that shit?"

The following afternoon, Femi and Monica were at *Phipp's* shopping for something to wear to Castle's All-White Birthday bash. His cocky ass rented out an entire hall, and hired photographers, press, and media to cover the event. Castle was taunting the Feds and he knew it.

"How do you expect your daughter to respect you when you can't even respect yourself?" Monica asked. "She's right, Femi. Your ass should've put your foot down long ago. The mothafucka had you tie your tubes just so he could stick his dick in other bitches. What fucking sense does that make? Then he got the nerve to have all these cars, houses, and businesses in your name. When the FBI finally reigns—and believe me they will—that piece of shit is gonna take you down with him. Your mother's probably rolling over in her grave."

Femi scoffed and shook her head. "You sound worse than Princess."

"You're my sister. I'm tired of seeing you put up with the bullshit."

Out of nowhere, Grip and Aviance walked up on them.

"Hey, wassup? What ya'll into?" Grip greeted.

"Trying to find something to wear to the party. Ya'll?"

"Shit, same."

Aviance hadn't stopped staring at Femi since they walked up. Her beauty had him stuck. "You two look nice today," he said, staring specifically at Femi. Her long, chocolate legs were on full display in a black romper. Those motherfuckers were greased up and looking right. If they were in private, he'd be on his knees spreading them apart, and lapping at her sweet pussy like a hungry, savage animal. Femi had a nigga whipped, and she didn't even know it.

The only person who seemed to notice him gawking was Monica.

"So I'll see ya'll tomorrow at the Defoor Centre, right?" Femi was asking both of them but she was looking directly at Aviance.

"Yeah."

"Fa'sho."

"Well, see ya'll then."

Femi and Aviance stared at each other longer than they should have. They were supposed to be keeping their affair on the low, but they were having a hard time keeping a straight, poker face.

Monica and Femi walked off together. As soon as the guys were out of earshot, Monica grabbed her arm and snatched her close. "You fucking that young nigga, ain't you?" she hissed.

"Of course not—"

"Stop lying!"

"Why you think I'm lying?"

"Bitch, 'cuz whenever you lie your voice gets high-pitched as fuck. I been knowing you damn near all my life, Femi."

"Monica, I—"

"Are you fucking him or not?"

Femi thought about lying, but it was no use. Her best friend saw through her every time. "Yes," she answered defeated.

Monica gasped dramatically. "How long?"

"Almost a year."

"Bitch, are you retarded? You gon' fuck around and get that kid killed—"

"No one knows...except you—and Princess."

"Your daughter knows?! Bitch, how messy can you be?"

"*Ssh*! Will you keep your voice down?"

"Femi, tell me you aren't this fucking careless?"

"What do you want from me? I'm only human. Don't I deserve some happiness? You see the way he looks at me. I miss those days when Castle used to look at me like that. I need to be needed, Monica."

"You gon' mess around and get somebody murdered chasing a memory. You need to pull the plug on that shit before your dirt catches up with you."

***

That day, Kirby decided to link up with Luna for answers. Castle insisted that he and Femi were separated, but she seriously had trouble believing it.

Kirby never intended to get cool with the baby mama, but it was obvious that she knew more about the situation. Luna even knew his wife's name. Kirby couldn't help but wonder what she and Castle's relationship was like. Was it different from what they had? Was Kirby really special? How many other women had he made broken promises to, and was he still with any of them? The unanswered questions kept Kirby up at night. She knew that she needed to meet with Luna again if she ever wanted to get to the bottom of shit.

After locating Femi's address through *peoplesmart.com*, they agreed it was finally time to pay Mrs. Black a visit. Kirby wanted the truth, and Luna felt it was finally time she met Castle's son.

Kirby was surprised by how close Femi's residence was to her apartment. McKenzie decided to tag along for the drama after her friend filled her in on everything. She was anxious to see how things would unfold.

Ironically, Femi lived less than fifteen minutes away from her. When Luna, Kirby, and McKenzie arrived at her home, Femi and Monica had just climbed out her G63. Collecting shopping bags from the backseat, they didn't notice the trio of younger women approaching them.

Kirby cleared her throat to make their presence known. "Are you Femi?" she asked, looking directly at her. She hadn't even seen pictures of her and she just knew the tall, beautiful, dark-skinned woman standing before her was Castle's wife.

Femi looked startled. She thought about grabbing the tiny pink pistol in her purse but realized they were just girls. She didn't bother asking who they were because she knew they were somehow related to her husband. They wouldn't be the first bitches to pop up on her doorstep uninvited. Femi tried her best to keep an open mind with chicks like them, but after 15 years her patience had run thin.

"Who the fuck is these hoes?" Monica said, rounding the truck. She had no issue whatsoever about choking a bitch.

"What do you want?" Femi asked with an attitude.

Luna stepped forward with her son in her arms. "We need to talk."

Femi looked down at the infant she was holding. She just knew eventually this day would come...

***

The sun had just set when Castle swaggered in him and Femi's home with shopping bags. He thought the materialistic shit was enough to keep her in love with him, when all she wanted was his time and attention. Sadly, she couldn't even get his commitment.

Castle locked the door behind him and punched in the code on the home security system. He then put the shopping bags off to the side. He'd dropped some bands at *Neiman Marcus* just to impress his wife, and hopefully put a smile on her face.

"Femi!" he called out. "Where you at, girl? Don't make me come lookin' 'round this mufucka for you."

As if on cue, Femi stepped into the foyer. She'd sent Monica home so she could deal with him without her instigation. A frown creased Femi's thick lips. Her eyes were red and puffy from crying. She wanted to stab his trifling ass after everything she learned.

"Wassup?" he asked confused. Castle knew something was wrong the minute he saw her. He knew that look all too well.

"Wassup is your fucking skeletons falling out the fucking closet! Mothafucka, you gotta son that you never even told me about!" Femi pushed him. "I'm your wife! How could you get some bitch pregnant behind my back and not tell me? You sat in my face and lied all those fucking times I asked you! How could you do some treacherous shit like that to me? *To me*?!" she stressed, tapping her chest. "Respect for your wife should be all the way across the fucking board! Then on top of that, I find out you fucking some lil' ass girl! That's what you want? A bitch that's practically your mothafucking daughter's age! What the fuck do you be thinking?" Femi punched his chest and then slapped him. "Answer me!" She went to slap him again, but he grabbed her hand in mid-strike. Femi quickly snatched away since she didn't want to be touched. She couldn't even look at his worthless ass. "What be going through yo' fucked up head to make you do the stupid shit you do!"

"Aye, calm the fuck down with all that shit!" Castle didn't care that she was his wife; he wouldn't tolerate any female hitting and hollering at him like they were crazy. "What the fuck is yo' ass even talkin' about?"

"Two bitches popped up with some lil' nigga claiming to be your son!"

"Whoooo?"

"Luna and Kirby! Yeah, nigga! You remember them? They told me everything. I'm not gon' to sit here and act like I don't know about the bitches but you dead ass wrong for not telling me about that baby—"

"Man, that lil' nigga ain't mine! I don't give a fuck about them hoes! All them hoes be lyin'! Look how I got you livin'. Look what I got you pushin'!"

"Nigga, I don't give a fuck out about this shit! And they can have the fucking ring 'cuz I'm done with you, Castle." Femi tried to walk around him but he grabbed her.

"Where the fuck is you goin'? Don't you ever in yo' life walk away from me."

Femi put up a weak struggle. "Move, Castle. I don't wanna do this shit with you. I'm tired," she cried. "I'm tired of all the bullshit. I can't take it no more. I'm done!"

"You my muhfuckin' wife, Femi. How we start is how we gon' finish. We not done 'til I say we done."

Femi tried to push Castle off, but he was too strong to battle. "How the fuck could you do me like that, Castle?" she screamed. "How could you have a fucking baby with a bitch and not tell me about it? You had me burn my fucking tubes!" Femi punched his chest. She wanted him to know and feel how much he'd hurt her. Nothing caused more pain than disloyalty and betrayal.

"I swear to God that bitch lyin', Femi! She just tryin' to pin the mufucka on me 'cuz she know a nigga caked up. I don't 'een know that bitch like that—"

"You lying! The baby looked just like yo' black ass! Be real!" Femi hollered. "Nigga, for once in your sad fucking life be honest!"

Castle backed Femi against the nearby wall. She was still talking shit when he pinned his body against hers. She tried to hit him but he grabbed her arms.

"Get the fuck off me, Castle! Don't touch me! I don't want shit to do with your trifling ass—"

"Aye, chill out. You know you ain't goin' nowhere. Fuck you gon' let two nobody ass bitches get in ya head?"

"Are they lying?" Femi demanded to know.

Castle kissed her tears away.

"I love the fuck outta you, Femi," he whispered.

"Castle, no...don't," she whimpered as he kissed her neck. She was telling him one thing, but she hadn't stopped him from unbuttoning her jeans either.

Pulling them down her legs, he dropped to his knees in front of her. Femi gasped when he licked her pussy from the outside of her panties. Next he snatched those off too. Femi didn't stop him when he gently took her clit in his mouth and sucked it. Using the tip of his tongue, he tickled her bud, and made it vibrate between his lips. Castle had mastered his head game. It was every one of his females' weakness.

"Oh, shit, baby. That feels sooooo good. You gon' make me nut," Femi moaned. Placing her hand on the back of his head, she fucked his face right there in the hallway.

"Bust in my mouth. I wanna see that pussy spray for a nigga." He flicked his tongue against her clit in fast-paced brush stroke motions. He made that motherfucker dance against her pussy, and every so often, he slipped his tongue inside.

"*Unhhh!*" she cried out. Femi could barely take it; her legs turned to jello as she trembled uncontrollably.

Castle stuck two fingers in her pussy and one in her asshole. Within seconds, she was jerking and squirting. Her fingernails dug into his scalp; he was trying to suck the soul out of her.

"Fuck me!" Femi begged. Little did she know, Castle wasn't going to stop until she pleaded for the D. He could eat the pussy for hours with no opposition.

Standing to his feet, Castle lifted her in his muscular arms and carried her to their bedroom. Once inside, he tossed her on the California king size bed and proceeded to undress. From the corner of her eye, Femi suddenly noticed Aviance's watch sitting on the nightstand in plain view.

Shit!

17

Femi quickly grabbed the watch and stuffed it under the pillows before Castle saw. He was the one who had brought Aviance the watch on his 20th birthday. If Castle had seen the Breitling sitting out in the open, he would've known Aviance was fucking his wife. Luckily, Femi was able to rob him of such knowledge. Castle would kill them if he ever found out the truth.

"Got my shit hard as fuck, bay. Get it wet fuh me," he said, stroking his staff.

Femi submissively crawled over towards him and took his rod in her mouth. After fifteen years, she knew just how he liked his dick and nuts licked and sucked on. Once his pole was good and polished, Castle climbed in bed and flipped her over.

"I'm finna give you what you need. 'Cuz this the real reason yo' ass trippin'. You been waitin' for a nigga to drop this dick off in you. Put that ass up," he ordered.

Femi was compliant as she arched her back and stuck it in the air. Castle didn't waste any time shoving his 11-inches inside. He loved how she was able to take it all. She never ran from the dick, and she even threw it back at a nigga.

"How this shit stay so gushy after all these years?" Holding onto her tiny waist, Castle stabbed her pussy from the back repeatedly like he had something to prove. When Femi's screams grew too loud she buried her face in a pillow. Her husband never made love; he punished the pussy.

Grabbing a handful of her hair, Castle gave it a gentle tug. "You love me? You fuckin' love me? Say you fuckin' love me!"

"I love you!" Femi screamed out.

"Fuck you thought you was goin'? Why you even playin'? You mine, Femi. I ain't ever lettin' you go."

***

After fucking Femi to sleep, Castle rushed out the house to call Luna. "Bitch, I'mma kill you!" he yelled into the phone. "Who the fuck you think you is pulling that shit? You must've lost yo' mufuckin' mind poppin' up at my wife's house!"

"Why didn't you tell her about us, Castle?"

"Bitch, I don't need to validate shit I do! You better pray I don't ring ya fuckin' neck when I see you!"

Castle hopped in his Rolls Royce and started the engine. He was on his way over to

Kirby's place since he had a few choice words for her simple ass too.

"So that's what it takes to make you come around?" Luna asked sarcastically.

"Bitch, don't fuck with me!"

"You fucked yaself! I should've made that visit sooner! You got these young ass hoes popping up at my house! You don't even take care of yo' fucking son—!"

"Fuck dat lil' mufucka! And fuck you too! Since you wanna bullshit, I got somethin' for both ya'll hoes. Let's see how well you fend homeless 'cuz you dead. Cut off. You hear me, bitch?"

Even though he wasn't active in their lives, Castle paid her rent faithfully because she didn't work. Unfortunately, Luna had no back up plan. If Castle took her home, then she and her baby would be ass out. Sadly, it was something she hadn't considered when agreeing to meet with Femi.

"All I ever asked was for you to take care of your son and be a daddy! You couldn't even do that, sorry ass nigga. Now you talking about putting us out? I wish you mothafucking would, Castle! Try me, and I will go to the courts *and* police on yo' stupid ass! Now play with it."

Click.

Castle pulled the phone away from his face and looked at it crazy. He paid her bills; that should've been enough. He couldn't believe Luna was trying to boss up on a nigga. She definitely had shit backwards. *Nah, this bitch ain't just say what I think she said.* As if he needed proof, Castle called Luna back. Surprisingly, she picked up on the first ring.

"Hoe, what the fuck you just let slip from yo' dicksucka?"

"Mothafucka, I ain't stutter! If you try to put me and CJ out I'll go to the police and tell them every fucking thing! I swear to God I will! "

Castle immediately made a U-turn. Kirby would have to wait. First he had to set Luna's monkey ass straight. "Yeah. *Unh-huh.* We'll see about that." He hung up on her and tossed his phone in the passenger seat. He couldn't get to her crib fast enough.

Twenty minutes later, Luna had just laid CJ down in his crib when someone came banging on her front door. She knew who it was without even having to look through the peephole. She pondered over the decision to let him in. He used to have a key, but since he never came around, she changed the locks being petty.

Back when she first got pregnant, Castle promised he'd be there for her physically and emotionally. Now that CJ was here, she couldn't even get the time of day. Castle didn't return her calls or text messages. He talked a good game in the beginning, but she soon realized that's all he was; talk. It wasn't fair for him to play house with Femi while she raised their son alone.

"Open the fuckin' door! Bitch, you hear me out here!"

Not wanting to rouse the neighbors, Luna rushed to the door and unlocked it. She barely had a chance to open it before Castle barged inside. He grabbed her throat and squeezed so tight that his nails dug into her skin.

"Yo' ass thought I was playin'?" he yelled. Spit sprayed onto her face.

Luna clawed at his hand, but there was nothing she could do to make him let go. Her eyes bulged in their sockets; she was unable to suck in air. If Castle didn't release his grip soon he was sure to kill her.

"Have you lost yo' fuckin' mind?! Bitch, don't ever in yo' mufuckin' life come at me on no hoe shit like that!"

Just when Luna thought the end was approaching, Castle threw her down on the floor. She immediately coughed and gasped for oxygen. The bruise on her neck would be there for days, but it was a small price to pay.

Castle stalked off in a huff, and Luna was left to wonder what he planned on doing next.

"Castle?" she called out in a hoarse tone. Struggling to stand to her feet, she followed him to the back of the apartment. Her heart dropped when she saw him snatch the 4-month old out the crib by his leg. "WHAT THE FUCK ARE YOU DOING?" she screamed frantically.

Luna tried to run at him, but he pushed her into the nearby wall. Determined to prove a point, Castle carried the tiny infant upside down and stepped out onto the patio. CJ cried hysterically the entire way. His father was heartless; cynical...but after today, Luna would never talk that cop shit again.

When she finally ran out on her balcony, Castle was dangling CJ over the rail by his leg.

18

"CASTLE, NO!" she cried. "Castle, no! No, Castle!"

"What was all that shit you was hollin' over da line?" he yelled. "You let that young bitch give you some nuts!"

"Castle, I swear I didn't mean it! You know I would never go to the police!"

"I'll drop this mufucka!"

Luna started freaking out. "Castle, I'm begging you!" she bawled. "Don't do this! I would never open my mouth about what you do! Please! Just give me my baby!"

Castle faked like he was about to drop CJ, and Luna damn near fainted.

"Castle, stop! Please! HE'S YOUR SON! *Oh, God*! God help me Please don't drop my baby!"

"Don't pray to God! Pray to me, bitch! I'm yo' mufuckin' God!"

Luna quickly clasped her hands together in prayer fashion. "Castle, please—"

"Get down on yo mufuckin' knees!" he demanded.

Luna willingly did as he commanded. "I'm begging you, Castle!" she cried. "I'm begging you...Please! Have mercy! He's your son! I'll do anything, Castle! I'm so sorry!"

Castle laughed heartlessly at her pitiful display. Satisfied with her humiliation, he finally raised the baby up. "Man, wasn't nobody gon' drop this lil' nigga."

Luna practically snatched her son from him. She hugged and held CJ closely while trembling. With all that happened she was still shaken up.

"I bet'cho ass don't talk that shit again," he said, walking past her. "Remember who you fuckin' with."

***

When you wake up before you brush your teeth....

You grab your strap, nigga...

Only time you get down on your knees...

Shooting craps, nigga...

Fuck what you heard, God blessin' all the trap niggas...

God blessin' all the trap niggas...

Castle's all-white birthday bash was live and in full effect that night. A red carpet was laid out at the front entrance, and photographers were on standby to snap photos. One would've thought an A-list celeb was in the building from the way Castle had shit set up.

"Swear dat nigga think he Big Meech or some shit," Aviance laughed. He and Grip were posted at the bar, away from the ruckus.

Castle and Femi mirrored Jay and Bey that evening. He was clean-cut in a crisp white Dolce and Gabbana suit with a salmon dress shirt underneath. The white Gucci crocodile loafers on his feet ran him about $2500. Femi looked dashing in a white strapless lace gown.

"Mufuckas dressed like they renewin' their vows or some shit."

If Grip didn't know any better he'd think Aviance was hating—when in fact he was just mad about seeing Femi on Castle's arm.

"Chill, bruh. It's the nigga's birthday."

Just then, Marissa walked over with a tray of jello shots. Everyone was so busy enjoying his or herself that no one immediately noticed the two uninvited female guests.

Kirby and McKenzie were the only ones present wearing red. She hoped it would make a statement.

Castle paid the radio station to advertise his event. McKenzie wound up seeing the flyer on Instagram. Neither Castle nor Aviance told them about the private shindig. It was obvious that they didn't want them there... Little did they know, Kirby and McKenzie had invited themselves.

Shuffling through the thick crowd of people, Kirby looked around for Castle. She finally spotted him over in VIP, hugging, kissing, and taking pictures with Femi. She just had to see it for herself. She just had to know if it was really true. Castle swore up and down they were separated, but she could see that was clearly bullshit.

So this is why he ain't invite me.

Kirby thought that shit was foul. He hadn't even mentioned his birthday bash once, and it was obviously because he wanted to celebrate it with his wife.

"This young bull be doing way too fucking much," McKenzie said over her shoulder.

Kirby thought she was commenting on Castle when actually she was glaring at Aviance from across the room. He was chitchatting with some bird that probably didn't even know McKenzie existed *or* that she was in Atlanta. McKenzie had no idea that he was speaking to Castle's 16-year old daughter. All she saw was a bitch that was all up in her man's face.

Kirby peered at Grip talking and laughing with Marissa. They hadn't spoken to each other since their last encounter back at her place. She automatically felt some type of way seeing them together. He also hadn't told her about the party for a reason.

Fuck him too, she thought.

Suddenly, Castle noticed Kirby and McKenzie from the corner of his eye. The fact that they were the only motherfuckers not wearing white was a dead giveaway. He almost shit bricks when he saw them walking towards him. *The fuck are they doing here*, he wondered.

Castle quickly departed the VIP section before Femi noticed Kirby. He wouldn't hear the fucking end of her mouth.

"What the fuck is you on, shawty!" he hissed once he reached her. If it weren't for them being in a public setting he would've choked her young, silly ass out.

"You fugasi, nigga. Why I ain't get an invite?" Kirby challenged.

"You been really showin' the fuck out. You gon' let these hoes get you fucked up," Castle said, looking specifically at McKenzie. He, like everyone else, always felt she was a bad influence.

"It was my idea to come. Now what?" Kirby was bucking because she thought he wouldn't hit her in public. Sadly, she was mistaken.

Castle snatched her up by her throat and squeezed. "Keep fuckin' with me, Kirby! I'll beat you and this bitch's ass!"

"Get the fuck off me!" Kirby shoved him.

Castle drew his hand back to slap the shit out of her, but Grip grabbed his wrist in mid-strike.

19

Castle looked up at his nephew like he wanted to spit venom at him. He'd never done anything that audacious before. If it weren't his birthday, Castle would've turned the fuck up, but instead of further making a scene, he straightened up his tux and pointed a finger in Kirby's face.

"Carry yo' mufuckin' ass home. I'll deal with you later."

Castle mean-mugged the shit out of Grip before turning and walking away. Kirby stood there speechless, on the brink of tears. She couldn't believe her man had dissed her at his birthday party because his wife was present. For the last three months he'd led her to believe she was the special, but now he'd just treated her like shit. Kirby loved Castle, and she didn't understand how he could be so cruel.

Monica stood several feet away. She'd witnessed everything, and couldn't wait to tell her girl what she saw.

"You good?" Grip asked Kirby. He hated to see her hurting. If he could, he would've gladly taken her burden.

Kirby cut her eyes at him in disgust. "Get the fuck away from me, Grip and go back to your bitch." Pushing her way past

McKenzie, she headed for the exit. To say she was embarrassed was an understatement. Kirby would never forgive Castle for the shitty way he behaved.

"What the hell is wrong with her?" McKenzie asked him.

Grip immediately went after Kirby to see if she was okay—and Castle peeped that too from his peripheral. When Grip finally made it outside, he tried to grab her arm from behind but she snatched away.

"Aye, chill the fuck out. I'm not the enemy, Kirby."

"Just go back inside and leave me alone."

Grip grabbed her wrist and spun her around to face him. It didn't take much effort considering her tiny frame. He hovered over her like a giant as he gazed into her beautiful brown eyes. Damn. She was so fucking pretty when she was angry.

Without thinking twice, he leaned down and covered his lips over hers. Kirby's body instantly tensed after his tongue pushed inside her mouth. As soon as one of his large hands went to her waist, she melted against his body. Her arms went around his neck, her fingers interlocking with his dreads. Their heartbeats were in sync as their tongues danced in unison. Every so often, he sucked and nibbled gently on her bottom lip. He wasn't even normally a biter, but something about her brought out the lascivious side of him.

Grip cupped her chin with his free hand as he increased the pressure. He needed her to know and feel how strongly he felt about her. When his lips moved to the side of her neck and behind her ear, Kirby stopped him.

"Grip...wait...we shouldn't," she whispered. "What if somebody sees us out here." Her lips said one thing but her brain said another. Her heart yearned for Grip even though he should've been off limits. They were playing it close and they knew it.

Standing in the over-capacitated parking lot outside Castle's birthday bash, they could've been caught at any moment. However, him finding out seemed to be the last thing on Grip's mind.

"I'on give a fuck. Let 'em see," he said in a hoarse voice.

Grip pulled Kirby closer. She was so small in his embrace. All he wanted to do was be there and protect her. Leaning down, he went in to kiss her again...

"Oh my God!" a voice said from behind.

20

Kirby quickly pulled away from Grip after seeing McKenzie and Aviance walk up. They'd caught an eyeful of their affection, and now the cat was out of the bag.

McKenzie looked from Kirby to Grip in shock. "*Unh-unh.* How long ya'll been doing this shit here?"

"Oh, you ain't know?" Aviance laughed.

It was obvious the two of them had kissed and made up. And Aviance was happy, because he was tired of watching Femi be all up under Castle. Femi didn't look very happy either to see him leave with McKenzie.

"What are ya'll asses doin' out here anyway?" Grip asked.

"We was finna zing to the store. What's your excuse," Aviance said.

"We weren't doing shit," Kirby lied. She could barely look them in the eye when she fibbed. Her cheeks were flushed and she was still hot and bothered from the kiss. If they didn't stop being so careless, people were sure to start speculating. Kirby was exhausted with all that had taken place. Turning to Grip, she asked, "Can you please take me home? I think I'm ready to go..."

***

Castle pulled his Maserati in front of his palace and Femi hopped out and slammed the door. He hardly had a chance to put the motherfucker in park. She was pissed after finding out one of his little whores had crashed the party. And to make matters worse, she was friends with Aviance's bitch.

Oh, the irony!

Femi's blood was boiling. Her night couldn't have gotten any worse. The celebration was still going on without Castle since she demanded he take her home after Monica broke the news. She could give a fuck about the guests and the party.

"Aye, calm the fuck down slammin' my shit."

"Fuck you!" Femi stormed inside the house and swung the door closed behind her. It almost flew into Castle's face after he rushed in behind her. "You foul as fuck for the shit you be doing!" she screamed. "How could you have that young hoe in there—with all our friends and family present! What the fuck do you be thinking?"

"That bitch was lookin' for trouble! You really think I'd do some stupid shit like that—"

"You do lots of stupid shit, Castle," Femi reminded him.

When he reached for her arm, she snatched away.

"Don't fucking touch me! I don't even wanna look at your black ass right now! I swear I'm hanging on by a thread, Castle. I'm sick of it! I'm sick of all the bullshit! All the bitches! All the lies! And now I find out you laying your seeds all across the fucking pond! I don't even know who the fuck I married anymore!"

"Femi—"

"Get the fuck out, Castle," she cried. Mascara ran down her cheeks as she bawled hysterically. She was really at her wits end with him. "Just get the fuck out. I need my space."

"So you just gon' kick a nigga out on his birthday?"

"Fuck your birthday, bitch."

***

Since Femi put his ass out, Castle wound up driving to Kirby's. He'd planned on staying the night, but first he wanted to give her little ass a piece of his mind. She was all the way out of line for the shit she pulled.

It was a little after 2 in the morning when he let himself in her apartment. McKenzie stayed the night with Aviance, who planned on dropping her off at the airport in the morning. The only people there were Kirby and her mother. Castle found her lying on the couch watching TV, but she quickly sat up when she saw him.

"I cannot believe you came here," she said, shaking her head. Kirby didn't want shit to do with him after the way he treated her tonight.

"Why the fuck wouldn't I? I live here, don't I? I pay the mufuckin' bills here."

"I don't know where you lay your head when you ain't with me, and honestly I don't care anymore."

"Fuck you mean?"

"You was wrong for the way you did me tonight. How could you not even invite me?"

"*She* put together that shit," he lied. "Fuck do I look like inviting my girl?"

Kirby surprised them both when she ran up and started hitting his chest. Tears poured from her eyes, she could no longer hold it in. "You a liar!" she screamed. "You're still with her! Yo' ass been lying to me all this fucking time!"

Castle slapped her crazy ass to the floor. "Bitch, don't ever in yo' life put yo' fuckin' hands on me!" he yelled. "I came here to try and make shit right, but fuck it. Sleep alone, silly ass bitch."

Kirby watched as he stormed out of the apartment and slammed the door behind him. She wouldn't dare go after Castle this time. Instead, she stood to her feet, grabbed her phone, and called Grip.

Surprisingly, he answered on the third ring. "Wus good?" He'd just gotten done dropping Marissa off. She threw a fit too. She'd wanted the D, but he wasn't really in the mood to deliver because he had Kirby on his mind.

"...Can you come through?" she asked.

21

Grip knew he shouldn't have answered his phone when Kirby called. He shouldn't have held her in his arms all night, and he shouldn't have sucked her pussy until she came and fell asleep.

When they awoke the following morning, Leah's caregiver attempted to cook them breakfast, but Grip peeled out. Things were getting real between him and Kirby, and he needed to put some space between them to clear his head. Falling for his uncle's girl was definitely not in the cards.

Kirby and Castle avoided each other the next few days following the incident since shit stunk for a few days. Normally, she was the first to throw the rope around and pull them together, but this time was different.

Kirby was happy when her girl, McKenzie flew back out the next weekend to celebrate her 18th birthday. Since she and Castle weren't on speaking terms, Kirby needed the company. McKenzie needed a break from Pennsylvania, so it was an even trade.

McKenzie's plane touched down at approximate 9:15 a.m., and she caught Uber straight to Kirby's address where she was greeted in the lobby.

"Happy birthday, *biiiitch!*" McKenzie sang. She looked cute that day in a baby blue floral mini sundress and sandals. She'd come dressed for the warmer weather down south.

Kirby laughed and they hugged like they hadn't seen each other in years even though it was only a week. "Thanks."

"How does it feel being 18 finally?"

Kirby shrugged. "I don't know. Kinda don't feel any different."

Together they walked up to Kirby's unit chatting the entire way. The first thing McKenzie wanted to know was if Aviance had been seeing anyone else that Kirby knew about. She was the jealous type who wouldn't hesitate to turn up if he misbehaved.

"Bitch, I don't be keeping up with that nigga. He's your man," Kirby laughed.

"True. I'll find out what I need to though. I always do. You know I don't be telling that nigga when I'm in town. I be trying to catch his ass slipping," she said. "So wassup with you and Grip?"

"Bitch, would you stop asking me about him. There's nothing going on between us," she lied. Grip was her little secret; she didn't kiss and tell. Kirby walked inside her unit and McKenzie followed.

"Yeah, whatever you say. Wow, it's nice in here. You changed it up a little I see," McKenzie said. Secretly, she was envious that it wasn't hers. Since she bullshitted for a living, it wasn't difficult at all to squeeze out the tiny white lie. Truth be told, she hated Kirby's new choice of décor.

She'd redecorated the home in hopes that it would make her feel better about the break up. She would do anything to get Castle out of her system. His lying ass hadn't called or texted in days.

"Thanks, boo. You can put your shit in my room. I've already got it made up for you."

Kirby proceeded to straighten up the living room while McKenzie made herself comfortable. "Damn, you redecorated the bedroom too?" she called out.

"Yeah, and the bathrooms."

After putting away her luggage, McKenzie roamed around Kirby's bedroom. She helped herself to the walk-in closet where she admired the variety of designer shoes. Castle had her spoiled. "So what we doing tonight? I know you trying to get lit for your 18th!"

"I heard something about Mansion on the radio the other night," Kirby called out from the living room.

Closing the closet door, McKenzie walked over to the dresser to survey her jewelry. Laying right in plain view was a $1500 diamond ring. McKenzie didn't think twice when she swiped it for herself. With all the shit Castle brought her she wouldn't notice...At least that's what McKenzie thought.

"I'm hungry as hell. You got anything to eat in this bitch?" she asked, walking out the room. "I'm mad I wasted ten dollars on that nasty ass sub on the plane."

"Bitch, I need to go shopping. I haven't had a chance to yet."

As though she needed verification, McKenzie opened her fridge and peeked inside. "Damn, bitch. This shit emptier than a fucking bowling alley."

"Bitch, I told you I needed to go shopping," Kirby said. "Look, why don't you just chill and make yourself at home. I'll run to Kroger and grab a few things. You want something?"

"*Ooh*, can you grab me some Naked drinks? The Red Machine and Blueberry kind."

"Yeah, sure."

"And some Twizzlers too!" she added just as her friend was leaving.

"Damn, bitch. Should I make a list?" Kirby joked.

"I promise, that's all."

After Kirby left, McKenzie plopped down on the sectional and turned on the TV. As usual, there wasn't shit on that interested her. She thought about watching reruns of *Love & Hip Hop* until she heard the front door unlock. Kirby wasn't even gone ten minutes.

"Damn, she got back quick."

Much to McKenzie's surprise it wasn't Kirby. Castle walked in carrying a bag from Saks Fifth, and the heavenly scent of Clive Christian. As usual, he was dressed in the finest designer wear.

Out of pure respect, he and McKenzie muttered curt hellos.

"Is Kirby back there?"

"No. She ran to the store real fast," McKenzie said.

"Cool. I'mma wait for her then." Castle placed the bag down by the door and plopped onto the sofa. He then pulled out a sack of weed and cigarillo. He thought about giving Kirby a few more days to calm down, but today was her birthday so he had to pull up. It was also time they made up after everything that happened. He hadn't seen her since his birthday.

Castle had a nasty habit of being too harsh on women, but it was only because of the way he was raised. He and Benny's father was a pimp and their mom, a prostitute. Seeing the way their father spoke and treated women somehow became natural to him. Castle had been desensitized to a lot of shit, especially the abuse. His fucked up upbringing only contributed to his lack of respect towards women. And now that he was close to pushing forty, it was far too late to change in his opinion. He was who he was. Any bitch could take it or leave it.

From the corner of her eye, McKenzie watched as he twisted up. Her pussy jumped when she noticed the way his tongue glided across the Dutch. All these months later, and she was still attracted to his fine, black ass.

Kirby don't even know what to do with all that. But I sure as hell do.

Her gaze traveled down to the area between his legs. Curiosity picked at her brain as she tried to figure out if he was holding or not. Kirby should've never left McKenzie alone with him.

Suddenly standing to her feet, she switched away and disappeared inside the bedroom. Less than a minute later, she reemerged and headed to the kitchen. She felt Castle's dark eyes on her the whole way there. He couldn't stop admiring her long, honey

220

brown legs. Up until now, he'd never paid any real attention to her. He usually liked his women with a little more melanin, but he would've been blind to not notice her game. Castle's dick sprang to life. From the way she was slanging that ass all over the place in her short dress he knew she was trying to get fucked.

"Would you like a bottled water or something while you wait?" McKenzie asked. "I think that's all that was in here." She opened the fridge and pretended to search even though it was practically empty. She also made sure to bend over extra hard so that Castle could see her bare ass. She wasn't wearing any panties and her kitty was shaved bald.

Just as she expected, Castle was watching and he certainly liked what he saw. He didn't think it was possible to get any harder. Yeah, McKenzie was definitely teasing a nigga. She knew exactly what she was up to. Castle wondered if she took her panties off when she disappeared inside the bedroom. If that was the case, she was clearly pressuring him. *Fuck it. If she throwin', I'm catchin'*, he reasoned.

Mashing the blunt into the ashtray, Castle slowly stood and approached her in the kitchen. McKenzie closed the fridge's door and reached for the cabinet. She was doing a poor job of pretending to be occupied. Suddenly, Castle grabbed the small of her back. He wasn't trying to waste any more time of play games.

"What are you doing, Castle?" she asked innocently.

"Shut the fuck up and bend over," he ordered. "Don't act like you don't know what'chu doin'..."

McKenzie happily obliged by leaning over the kitchen counter and tooting her ass up. Hearing Castle undo his jeans was music to her ears; she'd wanted the D for quite some time. Her curiosity brought about fantasies since Kirby never talked about their sex life. McKenzie didn't know it was because her friend was still a virgin. She, like everyone else, believed Castle was hitting that, but they were all wrong. Today was supposed to be the day he popped Kirby's cherry, but he was more interested in smashing her home girl.

Closing her eyes, McKenzie anticipated the moment when it first slid in. She expected him to ease in her pussy, but Castle spat in his palm, lathered his dick, and attempted to enter her ass. After several unsuccessful tries, he dropped down onto his knees and spread her butt cheeks apart.

"You gon' take some real nigga dick in this mufucka today," he told her.

McKenzie stifled a moan as his tongue maneuvered across her tight asshole. Her knees practically gave out when his tongue dipped inside. Castle was a freak. Unfortunately, she had little regard that he was also her best friend's man. "That feels so good," she whimpered. No man had ever licked her ass before. Most of the ones she dealt with acted like they were too afraid to even touch feet. McKenzie was positive that after today she'd be back for more.

Once she was good and moist, Castle stood and positioned himself behind her.

"*Unh!*" McKenzie gripped the edge of the counter to brace herself. Castle was so much bigger than she thought he'd be. "It kinda hurts."

"You was puttin' on like you wanted the dick now take it." Castle didn't even try to take his time as he tore her open aggressively. Her comfortableness was the least of his concerns. All he cared about was getting his nut off. "This what'chu flew down here for, ain't it?" Castle asked. "You been wantin' a nigga to hit. Now you got this big dick up in you."

McKenzie half-yelped half-moaned as he pumped into her from behind. "Oh, shit, Castle!" she cried.

"What? You thought I was gon' play with it?"

McKenzie let off a shrill whimper. The combination of pain and pleasure had her barely able to contain herself.

"Play with your pussy," Castle instructed.

McKenzie obediently did as she was told. Castle was definitely trying to turn her young ass out.

"Damn, I'm finna nut," he groaned. "You gon' catch it in your mouth?"

Before she could answer, he turned her around and forced her down in front of him. Castle made his dick spit all over her face and chest. Some of it even seeped into her eyes.

"Damn, you could've warned me you were gonna do that," McKenzie complained, wiping her irritated eye.

Castle quickly put away his flaccid penis and redressed. "My fault," he said nonchalantly. It was obvious he didn't give a fuck about her attitude or pink eye. "But look, I'm finna get up outta here. I gotta get home, wash the shit off my dick, and take care of some business," he said. "Tell Kirby I stopped by."

McKenzie was left in the kitchen to feel like a $2 hooker covered in semen. Castle couldn't have been any more rude and dismissive after getting his nut. And to make the situation worse, Kirby's mother had heard everything...

22

Aviance placed soft kisses along Femi's shoulder as they lay in a spooning position. They had just finished fucking in a deluxe king suite at the *Westin*. They used to smash at his crib, but she was always afraid of someone they knew seeing them. A lot of niggas he was cool with lived on his side of town as well as in his building.

Aviance had no idea that his girl McKenzie was back in town.

Not only did Femi need a nut, she also wanted someone to confide in about Castle's love child. She still had a hard time grasping the fact that he'd conceived a baby with someone else. Shaking her head, she said, "I still can't believe that dirty mothafucka betrayed me."

Aviance chuckled. "Fa real, Femi?"

"What?"

"You laid up with me right now, like what we doin' straight. Who betrayin' who?"

"That ain't the fucking point. This ain't about us, Aviance. It's about him and that baby he made with a bitch behind my back. And then to make it worse, he continues to lie about the shit. Like I couldn't see for myself the baby looked just like him."

"Did it really?"

Femi frowned and looked out her window at the skyline. Just talking about her husband put her in a sour mood. Castle thought the reconciliation sex had made her forget; he thought everything was good, but he was sadly mistaken. Femi had finally reached her breaking point with him. Enough was enough.

"I'm considering filing for a divorce," she admitted. "I even started looking at foreclosed homes to purchase. Thank God I have money saved after all these years of putting up with his ass. I can no longer tolerate the bullshit or the bitches. He can have it."

"Damn, bay. I hate you goin' through this shit. You know I got you if you need anything. That goes for Princess too."

Femi forced a weak smile. "Thanks."

"Speakin' of Princess...you don't think she'll say shit 'bout us to Castle, do you?"

Femi laughed. "Hell no. She hates that mothafucka more than anybody. She was more disgusted that I was sleeping with *you*, if anything."

Aviance joined in her laughter. With Femi being twelve years older than him, he could only imagine what that must've looked like to her daughter.

"Why Princess hate her pops so much?" he asked. The question had been bothering him for a while.

"He does it to himself. He's never around. He's too busy chasing money and underage pussy."

Releasing a sigh, he rested his chin on her shoulder. Aviance hated to see that she was so upset, but she knew what she'd signed up for when she said 'I do.' He wanted to take some of the weight off her shoulders. After creeping around for nearly a year, suddenly, the idea of being more seemed promising.

"Lemme ask you a question, Femi?"

"Wassup, A?"

Aviance paused. "Could you...I'on know...ever see us becomin' somethin' serious? If you really leaving the nigga I feel like I should be next in line."

Aviance was insulted when Femi broke out laughing. "Divorce my husband and be with you? Just like that?"

Aviance laughed. "Yeah, nigga." He felt foolish for even mentioning it. She never took him serious when he suggested them being a couple.

Femi hesitated for a second. "Aviance, I—"

"Fuck it...forget I even brought it up," he told her.

Femi could see that he was bothered, and she didn't want to hurt his pride any more than she already had. "Aviance...what we have...I'm cool with that. I mean, don't get me wrong, I love the time we spend. Behind closed doors it's cool, but in public that's a whole other story. On top of that, you're only twenty—"

"So you can get this dick, but I ain't man enough for you? That's what the fuck you sayin'." Aviance was offended.

"You know that's not what I'm saying."

He wasn't trying to hear that shit as he climbed out the bed. He was playing himself; it was obvious that Femi only wanted the dick. He didn't know why he thought something more could ever come from it. His paper was nowhere near as long as Castle's; neither was his wisdom. All he could offer her was realness.

"Nah, it's cool. I'm just the side dick. I get it." Aviance pulled on his True Religion jeans. "Go get you an ole' head."

"Don't be like that, Aviance. Come here. Get back in bed..." Femi patted the empty spot next to her.

Suddenly, Aviance's cellphone chimed indicating a text. After unlocking his iPhone, he read the message from Grip:

What's poppin for the nite?

Aviance quickly responded with:

Shit, it's whatever.

"Is that business?" Femi asked.

Aviance finished dressing and slid into his J's. "Yeah," he lied. "I'mma get up with you later, aight." Before Femi could argue, he was gone.

***

Future's *"Real Sisters"* anthem thumped through speakers inside *The Mansion Elan*. The popular nightclub was jammed packed that day with a few local celebrities sprinkled throughout.

Kirby and McKenzie were posted near the bar when McKenzie noticed a familiar face through the mass of people. "Is that...Aviance?" she tapped her friend's shoulder and pointed in his direction.

Kirby's eyes followed her finger. Sure enough it was McKenzie's boo with Grip and a few of their patnas in tow. Kirby couldn't believe they were all coincidentally at the same club.

"Yeah, that's him," Kirby said. She immediately looked for Castle out of pure habit, but didn't see him with them. She was supposed to be enjoying herself, but she was a little bummed out that he hadn't called and wished her a happy birthday.

Kirby didn't know that Castle had stopped over earlier. She also didn't know about the gift he'd left her because McKenzie stole that too. In Kirby's mind, Castle had completely forgotten about her and the realization hurt. What could he be doing that was more important than her birthday?

He ain't shit, she convinced herself.

McKenzie quickly pulled out her phone and called Aviance. From across the club, she watched him pull his out, look at it, and then shove it back inside his pocket.

Meanwhile across the club, Aviance was stalking his target like a predator to its prey. A cute dark-skinned chick with blue dreads and a fat ass had stolen his attention since she walked in.

Aviance tapped Grip's arm and pointed. "Man, that bitch so bad I'd let that hoe give me AIDS."

"You clownin'. That's some fucked up shit, bruh," he laughed.

Aviance slid up to her clique like he had a personal invite. He didn't give a fuck about interrupting the conversation she was having with her girls. "Wassup with you? You cute as hell."

"Thanks," she giggled.

"Shit, take down my math real quick. I ain't gon' be here long."

"You ain't gonna ask if we here with some guys?"

Aviance didn't miss a beat. "Honestly, I wouldn't give a fuck."

McKenzie's cheeks turned beet red when she saw him politicking with the small group of women.

"Oh hell no. That nigga straight tried to skip me," McKenzie said. "Come with me over there," she told Kirby. Since she couldn't fight worth a lick, McKenzie didn't want to risk going alone in case a confrontation popped off.

"Why?"

"'Cuz he still don't know I'm in town and I think it's time I announced my presence."

Grip and Aviance were shooting the breeze with the ladies when McKenzie and Kirby walked up. They had a good thing going too before they unexpectedly invited themselves, cock-blocking. Aviance almost spilled his purple drink when he saw McKenzie standing there in the flesh. He had his whole night mapped out, down to who he was going home with, before she appeared.

"Hey, Freckles," he greeted with a phony grin. "What'chu doin' here?"

"Hey, Freckles, my ass. You look surprised to see me," McKenzie smiled.

The chicks he was entertaining quickly dispersed after realizing he was taken. Aviance forced a smile like he was happy to see her. "When did yo' ass get here? And when were you gonna let me know?"

"I wasn't. I wanted to catch your ass in the act and I did." McKenzie snatched his plastic cup and took a sip.

"Why you over there lookin' mean, slim goodie?" Grip asked Kirby.

He'd lost an interest in the girls the minute she walked up. He hadn't taken his eyes off her since. Her hair was styled in loose body curls and her makeup was subtle yet flawless. The racy pink cut out dress she wore hugged her petite body in all the right places. He shouldn't have been staring that hard but he couldn't help it.

"I thought I wanted to step out tonight but I ain't really feeling it," Kirby said. She'd blown her mom off when she tried to tell her about Castle and McKenzie, because she was so anxious to get out. Now that she was finally out clubbing, she wasn't even enjoying herself.

Truthfully, Kirby was just depressed that Castle hadn't reached out for her birthday.

"Did you drive?" Grip asked her.

"No, we took Uber."

"Well shit, I was 'bout to get up outta here myself," Grip said. He and Aviance had been upstairs stunting in VIP for the last two hours, and he was burnt out and bored with the scene. Grip decided to throw all his cards on the table when he said, "You should slide with me."

"...And go where?" Kirby asked.

The fact that she didn't flat out deny him let Grip know where her head was. "Where ever. Don't matter..."

Kirby hesitated with an answer. "I don't know..."

"Tell you what? I'll be parked out front. I'mma roll a blunt. You got a few minutes. Think about it." With that said, Grip dapped up his boys and let Aviance know he was leaving.

"Aye, where you goin', bruh?" Aviance gave him a look that said *so you just gon' leave me here with this bitch*.

"Prolly to the crib. I'mma get up with you later though, aight?" Grip had no sympathy for Aviance or his drama as he walked out of the club solo.

When Kirby looked back over at McKenzie she was all in Aviance's face, trying to reassert her dominance. Since her girl was preoccupied, she figured *what the hell*. McKenzie would be the first one to say YOLO.

Kirby quickly slipped away from the altercation before they could involve her. On her way out, she sent a brief text message to her friend: ***I'm gonna have Grip take me home. I'm not really feeling it. I'll see u later***.

Kirby found him parked out front in his tank. It was freshly waxed and the rims polished to perfection. Running a hand through her curled hair, she stared at his G-wagon for several seconds. Kirby knew he was watching her through the tinted windows, patiently waiting for her to make her move.

If I get in this truck, she thought to herself.

Kirby could walk away, but she knew that wouldn't erase her attraction or interest. Swallowing her fears, she headed over towards his vehicle. Grip politely reached over and opened her door. She quietly climbed inside before fastening her seatbelt. Neither said a word to each other immediately. Instead they sat in total silence, attempting to read the other's thoughts. Flashbacks of him dipping his head between her thighs came to mind, and she had to cross her legs.

"It's my birthday," Kirby finally said

"Word? Happy birthday, ma. Why you ain't tell me earlier? We could've planned somethin'."

The truth was, Kirby was hoping Castle would come through, but as usual he was a huge disappointment. Grip pulled on his blunt a few times before passing it to her. Normally, she wouldn't have, but that time she accepted. "Don't feel like it though..."

Grip switched the gears to drive and pulled off. "Let's change that then," he said.

Half an hour later, Kirby was wearing a look of pure confusion. "Why are we at the airport?" she asked.

Grip had just parked his truck on the top tier of the parking garage. He had something up his sleeve, and he hoped she went along with it. "Just trust me, aight."

Kirby had her reservations, but she still followed him inside the crowded Hartsfield-Jackson. "Grip, what are you up to?" she laughed. Kirby had to jog a little just to keep up with his fast-paced walking. He was on a mission.

Out of nowhere, Grip stopped, and turned towards her. She didn't expect him to lean down and kiss her lips. His hands immediately went to her tiny waist as he pulled her close. She was so small that his large palms nearly wrapped completely around her midsection.

Kirby stood on her tiptoes to savor the breathtaking kiss. A moan escaped her throat as he lightly caressed the length of her arm. He was both aggressive and passionate. His kiss was ravenous; his groans and touches animalistic. For a second, she thought he might actually take her right there in the airport.

Castle could've been standing less than several feet away and they still wouldn't have stopped. "What are we doing?" she whispered, winded.

Grip's jaw muscle tensed. He knew that he was being reckless, but to him Kirby was worth the risk. "Finishing what we started..."

23

She was the baddest, I was the realest...

We was the flyest, up in the building...

Countin' this money, lovin' the feelin'...

Look at you now, in love with a hitta...

"*All Eyes On You*" poured the speakers of the rented Mercedes E350 Convertible. Two hours after touching down, Kirby and Grip were cruising through Miami Beach with the top missing headed to *Fontainebleau*.

"Oh my God. I can't believe I'm here, Grip. This is crazy."

He was happy that he could put a smile on her face. Now that they weren't in Atlanta, they could kick it without people they knew seeing them. For tonight and tomorrow, Kirby was his.

When they first arrived at the hotel, concierge tried to hassle them about reservations. Grip was able to talk them into making an exception after sliding them a few Franks. They secured a beautiful suite overlooking the beach. As soon as they stepped inside, Kirby's phone started blowing up. It was McKenzie.

"She probably wondering where I'm at," she laughed. "She's supposed to be staying at my place while she's in town." Kirby was just about to answer but Grip took her phone from her.

"Fuck that. Aviance got her. They all gon' have to wait." Grip powered off her phone and removed the battery to let her know how serious he was. Kirby watched him toss both pieces on a nearby chair. He then pulled her towards him. "I got'cho' mufuckin' ass now." Grip leaned down and gently bit her bottom lip, giving it a little tug with his teeth. She thought they were about to get it popping, but he walked off towards the kitchen. "They left us a gift," he said, picking up the complimentary bottle of wine. "You drink, right?"

Kirby gave him a flirtatious look. "Not really...but tonight I been feeling daring..." She didn't know what it was about Grip, but he brought out the bad girl in her.

"You gon' fuck around and get fucked talkin' like that," he warned her. Kirby laughed even though he was dead ass serious. The expression on her face said 'yeah right', but she had no idea what Grip had in store for her.

Kirby kicked off her heels and took a seat on the ivory sofa. "So what are we gonna tell people when they realize we're gone?"

"We ain't gon' worry about that shit right now."

Grip poured them each a generous amount of wine before joining her in the living room. He was surprised to discover Kirby stretched out naked on the sofa when he walked inside. She was ready.

Placing the drinks down, he slowly approached her. "Get up."

Kirby sat up, Grip took a seat beside her, and in one fluid motion he placed her on top of him in a straddling position. His hands explored her firm body before settling on her ass. Kirby responded by pulling his t-shirt over his head. His diamond chains glistened against his black wife beater. Next Kirby took off his hat and removed his rubber band. Once his hair was free, she ran her fingers sensually though his long dreads. That shit drove him crazy.

Grip bit his bottom lip and sighed. Kirby had him hard as hell. "Yo' lil ass tryin' to get bust down, ain't 'chu?"

Kirby kissed him with fervent urgent need. Pressing her fingers in his abs, she grinded sensually against his erection. He thrust slowly from underneath, brushing against her clit.

Grip lifted Kirby up so that her knees were on the back of the sofa and her crotch was buried in his face. He knew that as soon as he took a taste he would never have enough. His mouth covered her sopping pussy. He sucked on her clit like he was parched, determined to make her cum so hard that Castle became irrelevant.

He ate her pussy so good that Kirby found herself grabbing and pulled on his dreads. Grip made her ride his tongue when he lifted her entire body up and down as if he were bench-pressing. At 120 lbs., she was easy to manhandle and maneuver. He rotated between tongue fucking her hole and French-kissing her clit.

"Cum on my face," he ordered. "I wanna taste dat mufucka…"

Shrill whimpers bounced off the hotel room's wall. Her body trembled uncontrollably as she bucked against his mouth. The overwhelming pleasure he created was unbearable. Her toes curled and her body shivered. Kirby attempted to retreat, but Grip mannishly squeezed her ass to hold her in place. The harder she tried to run the more vigorously he sucked on her button.

"Oh, shit, Grip! *Oooooohh!*" she squealed.

No longer able to hold himself back, he stood and carried her to the bed. After gently laying her down on the pillow top mattress he proceeded to slowly undress. As he stood there fully nude, Kirby took in every beautiful tattoo on his rich caramel skin. His six-pack met right above his V-cut, which led to a curly mass of public hairs. In the center was thick 9-inches of curved wood with a faint birthmark on the tip.

Grip was surprised when Kirby boldly took him in her mouth. She sucked and stroked him at the same time, occasionally running her tongue across his nuts.

"Damn, girl...shit," he groaned. Moving his dreads from out of his view, Grip watched as Kirby polished his dick with her lips like an expert. Castle would kill her if he knew she was blessing another nigga with the head skills he'd taught her. "I ain't finna play with yo' ass. Lemme put this birthday dick up in you..." Grip softly pushed her back on the bed, and slid between her legs.

"Grip...hold on...I gotta tell you something—"

Ignoring her statement, he tried to stuff the head in, but stopped after she winced. Kirby saw the confusion on his face; he was startled by the fact that she was still a virgin.

Grip looked in her eyes and saw fear and trust. Grabbing her legs, he pulled them tighter around his waist. Kirby nervously looked down, but he cupped her chin and tilted her head up. "Look at me," he told her. She did, and he kissed her deeply. Her mouth opened to his, and their tongues met for a brief moment. "Can't let that nigga have you now," Grip said. And he meant every word of that shit.

Kirby winced when he pushed his head against her center.

"*Ssh. Ssh*," he whispered in her ear. Grip softly kissed the side of her neck and collarbone. Her fingernails dug in his back after he broke through the first layer of muscle. "Relax, and let me in, bay. I'mma teach you how to take this dick."

"It hurts a lil'…"

"Relax for me, baby…"

Kirby tried to ease up, and after several thrusts he finally pushed through. The pain slowly subsided and pleasure soon took over in its place. Grip made sure to take his time as he stroked her. Teasing her a little, he pulled out every now and then and rubbed the tip against her clit. "You so fuckin' tight, and wet." Grip gently slid back inside.

Kirby's hand went to his 6-pack. "Don't cum—"

He quickly grabbed and moved it. "Fuck that. I'mma nut in *my* pussy."

Kirby whimpered in pleasure.

"I fuckin' mean it…That nigga can't have you…"

***

"So have you thought more on what we talked about?" McKenzie asked. It was a little after 5 a.m. and the sun was just beginning to peak over the horizon. They were at Aviance's loft in Old Fourth Ward. After fucking she couldn't wait to bring up her scheme again.

Aviance pinched one of her nipples. "'Bout what?"

McKenzie sat up in bed and looked at him crazy. "You know damn well what."

"About you gettin' my name tatted on you?"

"I'm not talking about that," she said.
"That mufucka would look good on you," he laughed.

McKenzie slapped his hand away. "Aviance, I'm serious," she told him. "You know what I'm talking about."

He sighed in frustration and turned away. "You still tryin' to get me to rob my nigga?"

"Think about it. You ain't gotta answer to that arrogant mothafucka no more. *You'd* be the man. You can start your own business...maybe somewhere low-key like Arkansas. I got some niggas in Philly who'd help with the lick for a cut. Ya'll can hit the trap houses together, and by the time Castle finds out, we'll be long gone."

"*We*? What'chu mean *we*, Freckles? You sayin' the shit like you down to start over with a nigga."

"This is *my* plan. I'm taking this journey too. I'm with you, Aviance. We're in this shit together."

Aviance admired her loyalty and valor. It was why she was still in his life. She wasn't like a lot of young chicks. Leaning in, he kissed her lips then her neck. He had nothing to lose. She was right. He would never have Castle's money or status unless he took off and did his own thing. Femi would never take him seriously; she'd made that more than clear during their last time together.

"Wassup? Are you down or what?" McKenzie pressed.

Aviance reached over and grabbed a small silver tray off the nightstand beside the bed. She watched as he snorted a couple lines before passing her the dish. McKenzie went ahead and indulged as well.

Aviance sniffled dramatically and wiped away the residue on his nostrils. "Fuck it," he said. "I'm wit' it. Let's rob the nigga..."

***

Sunlight streamed through the curtains in their suite, waking them the following morning. Grip smiled when he opened his eyes and saw Kirby. Even with crust in her eyes she was beautiful.

"I can wake up to this face every day," he told her.

"Really?"

He laughed. "Yeah, nigga. Really."

Kirby grinned, showing off the small gap between her front teeth. That was one of his favorite things about her. "But I ain't got no makeup on," she whined.

Grip chuckled. "It's cool. I ain't got no makeup on either, so we even."

Kirby laughed before hitting him with a pillow and kissing him. After pulling back, she tilted her head and studied his features. "You know what? You kinda look like Castle...just lighter in complexion."

Grip sucked his teeth. "Aight, get the fuck out my face now, buster." Since he wasn't trying to hear that shit, he playfully mushed her.

That morning Grip fed hesr fruit in bed. They horsed around, laughed and talked about everything under the sun. She'd been with Castle three months, and she felt more of a connection with Grip than she ever did with him.

After a brief 69 session and shower together, they strolled hand in hand on the beach. For lunch, they ate Italian on a lake and fed the breadcrumbs to birds. Kirby was enjoying herself so much with Grip in Miami that she got depressed whenever she thought about going back.

Their dessert had just arrived when his cellphone vibrated on the table. He and Kirby looked down at it simultaneously. Much to their dismay it was Castle. Grip released a sigh of frustration. His uncle always did have the worst timing. He went to grab his phone but Kirby quickly stopped him.

"Don't answer it."

Grip looked down at her small hand covering his. She smiled and it melted his heart. "Like you told me yesterday...they can wait."

24

Kirby didn't expect to come home to a quiet house the next afternoon. She figured McKenzie was staying with Aviance temporarily, because she hadn't called again. Kirby found her mother resting in her bedroom. Her caregiver had actually dozed off in the recliner next to her bed. Lightly tapping her shoulder, Kirby let her know that she was relieved for the day.

"How you feeling?" she asked Leah.

"Tired," her mom said, sitting up. "Where you been? It's not like you to take off without calling."

"I know. I'm sorry. Something unexpected came up," was all she said. Thoughts of Grip between her thighs came to mind, and she quickly shook them away. "McKenzie, ain't been here?" Kirby asked.

"I haven't seen her since the night ya'll left..." Leah grimaced. "And speaking of her, I got something to tell you about your lil' friend..."

Kirby took a seat on the edge of Leah's bed. Her eyebrows knitted together as she patiently waited for her mother to continue. "What is it, ma?"

"Well...the other day—your birthday to be exact—I heard her and Castle in the other room f—"

She was suddenly interrupted by the sound of the front door opening. Daddy was home. "Hold on, ma," Kirby said. She quickly hopped off the bed and rushed to the front of the apartment.

Castle swaggered inside looking like a million dollars. On his feet was a brand new pair of red high top Giuseppes. A Versace tee hugged his broad chest, and a pair of navy blue J. Crews hung off his waist. He didn't look happy when he closed and locked the door behind him.

"Fuck you been at? And why you ain't been answerin' my mufuckin' calls?" he hounded.

Kirby folded her arms and frowned. "You got some fucking nerve, for real. Don't come for me. You didn't even call or stop by to see me on my birthday—"

"Fuck is you talkin' 'bout? I did swing by. Yo' ass wasn't here. Yo' peoples ain't tell you? I even left you a lil' present."

Kirby shook her head in disgust. Castle was pathetic, and she was positive that he was lying. "I ain't get shit, nigga. Not even a fucking text."

"Well, I know what the fuck I did. I don't know what the fuck to tell you, baby girl. Anyway where was yo' ass these last two days?" He loved to turn the tables to take the focus off of him.

"I went to visit Kaleb," she lied.

"You ain't asked me if that was cool."

"Castle, get the fuck outta here. You got your own fucking kids, and I ain't one of them." Kirby was feeling herself, but he quickly reminded her who he was when he slapped her.

"You better chill the fuck out, lil' girl. Yo' ass done went MIA and came back bold as fuck. I ain't ya mufuckin' brother. Act like you know a nigga."

Kirby grabbed her stinging cheek and backed away from him. "That's the thing! I don't!" she screamed. "We supposed to be living together but you hardly ever here! All you do is cheat and lie! I don't know what to fucking believe anymore."

"Man, yo' ass trippin'. I'll come back when you out yo' feelings." Castle started to leave, but Kirby grabbed him by the back of his shirt.

"Don't fucking walk away from me!" she screamed.

Castle whirled around and slapped the shit out of Kirby. She dropped instantly after the vicious blow. "What I tell yo' fuckin' ass about touchin' me!" he brutally kicked her in the ribs to let her know who was in charge. "I ain't the fuckin' one, bitch!"

"Get away from her!" Leah weakly shoved Castle and smacked him with what little strength she had.

Kirby was cowering on the floor when her mother came to her rescue. She was surprised to see the frail woman on her feet.

Castle backed up in shock. He couldn't believe Leah had actually put her hands on him after everything he'd done for her. He'd paid off her debt and moved her and her ungrateful daughter out the decrepit home they lived in. Now this was the thanks he got.

When Kirby saw him ball his fists, she quickly scurried to her mom's defense. She'd die before she let him hurt her sick mother.

Castle looked from Kirby to Leah. He was tempted to whup both their asses but he decided to spare them. "Fuck you and that bitch!" he said, turning to leave. The door slammed loudly behind him, and she heard Castle punch the hallway wall in anger.

All of a sudden, there was a light thud behind her. Kirby quickly turned around and realized her mother had fainted.

"MA! Ma, what's wrong?" Kirby rushed to her mom's aid. From what she could see, Leah was not breathing. "Castle!" she screamed. "Castle, wait! Come back! I need you! Something's wrong with my mama! *CASTLE*!"

Sadly, he didn't come back, and Kirby was left alone to tend to her dying mother.

***

Grip was with Aviance when Kirby called and told him she was at the emergency room. They were on their way to the bar, but he made an immediate U-turn and headed straight to the hospital. They found her in the waiting room livid and in tears. As soon as she saw Grip, she hugged him and buried her face in his chest. Her mom was pronounced dead twenty minutes ago.

"How could I be so fucking selfish, Grip?" she cried. All the time wasted chasing after Castle should have been spent with her mom. Now it was too late.

"Aye, it ain't yo' fault. You hear me? Don't ever blame yaself, Kirby."

Aviance stood off to the side as Grip comforted Kirby in her time of need. Castle should've been there to console his girl but instead the nigga was probably out somewhere chasing skirts. Castle didn't know it, but Aviance had something planned for his callous ass.

"Do you need anything?" Grip asked Kirby on the way to her apartment. She hadn't said a word since they left the hospital and he was concerned about her. He knew her brother was locked up and her mom was all she had.

"Rest. Just rest," she said. When Grip finally pulled up to her apartment building, Kirby turned around and looked at Aviance in the backseat. "Can you do me a favor and not break the news to McKenzie? Right now I just need a few days to myself."

"No doubt," he said.

Grip watched her unbuckle her seatbelt and slowly climb out. There was so much he wanted to say to her; so much he wanted to do to comfort her...but he didn't know where to start.

Grip stopped her right before she climbed out. "Kirby? Stay up aight? I got'chu if you need anything. Anything," he stressed.

"Thank you, Grip. I appreciate everything."

After Kirby hopped out, Aviance jumped in the front seat. Grip didn't pull off until he made sure she was safely inside.

Kirby called and texted Castle for the next few days, but he never answered. She couldn't believe how easy it was for him to turn his back on her when she needed him. He knew that her mom passed away, and she needed money for a proper burial. Kirby didn't work, and she didn't have much saved up. Unfortunately, she'd put all her eggs in one basket with him. She thought he'd always be there for her, but apparently he had fed her a bunch of bullshit.

Thankfully, Grip came through and paid for a beautiful service at Ebenezer Baptiste Church. The service was small with only a few people showing to pay their respect. Kirby was surprised when Castle didn't show up. Knowing him, he was probably buried in some bitch's pussy. It was fucked up because she really needed him during her time of mourning. However, it was clear that he didn't give a fuck about what she was going through.

If it wasn't for Grip, Kirby didn't know if she would've survived it all. It was supposed to be Castle offering financial and emotional support, but his nephew quickly picked up the slack.

Aviance and McKenzie were among the people who came to pay their respect. As soon as Kirby saw her best friend walk in, her mother's last words came to mind.

She and Grip were standing near the front pew when McKenzie approached her teary-eyed. "Kirby, oh my God," she cried. Kirby stood stiff as a board as her friend hugged her tightly. "I'm so sorry! Why didn't you call me? Why didn't you tell me when it happened? Why did I have to find out from Aviance a day before the funeral? We're sisters, I could've been there for you—"

Out of nowhere, Kirby hauled off and punched her dead in the face. The few people in attendance gasped in shock. No one expected the devastating blow—especially McKenzie. Her nose started leaking immediately after.

"What the fuck is your problem?!" McKenzie screamed.

Blood seeped into her mouth and stained her teeth. She couldn't believe Kirby had hit her. Everyone stared at her like she was crazy, but she didn't care. The few days she took piecing together what her mom tried to tell her had finally led to this moment. Since the beginning, Leah had preached to her about the company she kept, but Kirby just wouldn't listen.

Grip quickly grabbed her up from behind and carried her out of the chapel, kicking and screaming.

"You ain't my fucking sister, bitch! You dead to me!"

***

"Why you do that shit back at the funeral?" Grip asked. "Last time you'll ever get to see ya moms and you do that ratchet shit." He could never imagine himself doing something like that at his own parents' funerals. Kirby should've practiced restraint.

He didn't take his eyes off the road as he navigated his truck. They had just left the cemetery, and Kirby hadn't said a word since her outburst at the funeral home. Needless to say, neither McKenzie nor Aviance were present for the burial. Luckily, Grip was with her every step of the way. And while he hated to pry, he had to know why she flipped on her girl like that.

Kirby didn't respond. She stared out her window at the passing scenery completely lost in thought. She couldn't believe her mom was actually gone. Kirby knew the day would eventually come, but she wasn't prepared for it. Kaleb was in prison when he should've been there. Everything was fucked up.

"Kirby..." Grip didn't want to have to repeat himself. If he planned on supporting her then he at least deserved to know what was going on inside her head. "Why you buck like that back at the service? You know that ain't you."

"...She deserved it," Kirby simply said.

***

"Why ole' girl flip out like that?" Aviance asked.

McKenzie was standing at his bathroom sink with her head tilted back and bloody tissues balled up in her hand. Her shit hadn't stopped leaking since the funeral. She couldn't tell him it was probably because Kirby found out she'd fucked Castle.

"I don't know. She just fucking went postal. If her mama ain't just die, I would've whupped her ass," she lied. McKenzie knew damn well she couldn't scrap. "For a while, I think she been jealous of our relationship since Castle be dogging her so much. Maybe that coupled with the stress of her mom dying made her snap."

"I ain't even know she had that shit in her. She always seemed so chill."

"Everybody got a breaking point, I guess..."

25

"Fuck yo' ass been these last few days?" Castle asked Grip the next afternoon. He and a few of their patnas were playing pool at *Benchwarmer's* on Clairmont Road. This was his first time seeing his nephew since the birthday party. Grip was obviously staying out the way. Castle didn't like feeling as though he were being avoided.

Grip focused on his shot with his back to his uncle. The nigga would flip if he knew he'd smashed Kirby and had her holding zips first. "I been chillin' with Marissa," he lied.

Castle took a swig of his beer and shook his head. "That hoe just a fine ass setback," he said. "Money talks and bullshit takes the bus. Remember that business should always be top fuckin' priority."

"Damn, nigga. I *do* have a life," Grip retorted.

Castle's smirk immediately vanished. He hadn't been digging Grip's attitude or cockiness lately. "Aye, lemme holla at you outside real quick, playa."

Grip attempted to take a shot and missed. Castle had fucked up his concentration. After placing the pool stick down, he followed his uncle out to the parking lot. Once they were standing in between two vehicles, out of plain sight, Castle snatched his gun out and shoved it in Grip's face.

"Mufucka, you really been tryin' me up," he said with a menacing stare.

There was no trace of fear in Grip's eyes as he held Castle's intense gaze. The normal person would've panicked from his unexpected actions, but it'd take more than a loaded pistol in his grill to make him frighten.

"You think I don't know about you, mufucka? You think I ain't been noticin' the lil' shit you been doin'? You ain't slick, mufucka. Yo' ass think I don't know you want my bitch?"

Grip didn't blink or flinch. If it weren't for Castle being his uncle, he would've broken his jaw. "Nigga, if you ain't gon' squeeze, get that mufuckin' gun out my face."

Castle glared at his nephew but slowly lowered his weapon. He saw so much of himself—and Benny in him. Grip was cut from the same cloth. He didn't cave easily like a lot of niggas. Castle wasn't fucking with him, but he did admire his brazen frankness.

"I'm warnin' you, mufucka," he said. "Stop testin' me. You don't wanna get on my bad side."

***

Kaleb lit a Newport as soon as he stepped foot outside the prison walls. Finally, after two and a half years, he was a free man. Standing beyond the tall metal gates of the penitentiary he wore the same outfit he'd been arrested in back in 2012. A white T-shirt and Levis. He was barefoot at the time of his arrest, but fortunately the staff allowed him to keep his tennis shoes.

Kaleb's P.O. Jasmine picked him up in her 2014 BMW. She was a short, thick coffee brown sister with light gray eyes. When he climbed inside her car, she had several shopping bags filled with clothes and shoes in the backseat. Jasmine spent a pretty penny.

"Hey, baby. I didn't know what you liked to wear so I got you a little bit of everything."

"Good lookin'."

Kaleb tossed his stale cigarette out after Jasmine handed him a freshly rolled blunt. He'd been fucking with her since he got knocked. She was crazy about a nigga even though he was 17 years younger than her. Her colleagues would've frowned upon what she was doing if they knew, but she didn't care. Kaleb was bae.

"What are we doing tonight to celebrate your release?" Jasmine asked excitedly. "I was thinking we could go—"

"I can't fuck with Philly right now, ma. I gotta get to my sister." His expression was blank as he stared straight ahead, and his disposition bleak. He knew his moms had passed and his sis was alone in Georgia. He didn't give a fuck that he was on probation and couldn't leave the states. Kirby needed him.

Jasmine looked disappointed but she wouldn't dare oppose. As a matter of fact, she was down to cover for him if need be. She was a loyal ride-or-die. "Okay. Do you need anything?" she asked.

Kaleb fired up the blunt and inhaled. "Your car, a lil' cash, and some pussy."

***

The following afternoon, Castle pulled up on Kirby and called to tell her to come downstairs because he had a surprise. When she walked out of her building she found him parked in front inside a brand new pearl white Mercedes Benz with chrome rims. It was her dream car.

Castle hoped the gift was enough to get back in her good graces, but he was wrong. He didn't expect Kirby to fold her arms and glare at him.

Hopping out the whip, he closed the door and tried to hand her the keys. "Hey, baby. I got'chu somethin'. I heard what happened and I thought this might cheer you up."

"*Cheer me up?*" she repeated. "Nigga, I needed your support when my mama died, not a fucking car! You can take those keys and shove 'em up your black ass!"

"Come on, baby girl. Don't be like that. A nigga figured you needed your space—"

"Did you fuck McKenzie?" she blurted out.

Castle looked shocked by her accusations. He never thought that skeleton would fall out of the closet. "Hell naw!" he lied. "Why would you ask me some shit like that, baby? That bitch ain't 'een my type."

"My mother said—"

"Yo' moms always hated a nigga and you know that shit. She lied to you if she told you that bullshit. God rest her soul...I hate to say it, but she wanted to see us split before she died—"

"Don't you dare stand in my face and call my mother a liar."

"I would never smash that bitch. On my soul. You know I love and care about you. Why the fuck would I do some weak shit like that? What type of nigga you think I am, baby girl?"

Kirby narrowed her eyes. She was actually starting to believe him. He definitely looked sincere. She never thought they'd be capable of doing something so foul. But being hopeful and being naïve were two very different things.

"The same reason you lied about having a wife and kids," she said.

"I told you me and that bitch ain't 'een together. Matter fact, I already filed the papers."

"You lie so much, Castle."

He slowly walked over to Kirby and pulled her close. The fact that she didn't fight with him let him know she still loved him. She was talking that shit but she wasn't going anywhere. "I'm not lying. Look, I know I fucked up by not being there for you. I'm sorry about ya moms. And I swear from here on out I'mma do better. I put that on everything. It's me and you, Kirby."

26

Kirby ended up taking Castle's lying ass back like she always did. With her mother gone, she felt like she needed him now more than ever to fill the void. He wasn't shit half the time, but he was the only real person she had in her corner.

Castle tried to butter her up by having professional caterers come to the house and prepare a candle lit dinner that evening. He wanted to make up for lost time and the fact that he wasn't there for her when Leah died. That night, if she was up to it, he planned on finally putting some dick in her back.

They had just taken their seats at the dining room table when someone knocked on her apartment door.

"You expectin' company?" Castle asked, somewhat agitated. He'd gone to great lengths to have the perfect date, and now someone was interrupting it.

"No. I wasn't. But I'll answer it." Kirby stood and made her way to the door. After unlocking the bolts, she swung it open without looking through the peephole first. Her mouth practically hit the hardwood floors when she saw her brother standing there in the flesh.

Kaleb had driven to Georgia with few breaks in between just to come and take her home. One of the C.O.'s he used to smash had a private property she promised to him upon his release. A young pimp at heart, Kaleb had all types of bitches looking out for a nigga.

Kaleb stepped back and surveyed his sister. Kirby didn't look like the same little girl he remembered. There was something different about her and he knew it had a lot to do with Castle.

"Kaleb! Oh my God! It feels like I'm dreaming! Are you really here? When did you get out?" Kirby flung her arms around his neck with such force that she almost knocked him off his feet.

"Yesterday," he said. "Why you got all this shit caked on yo' face?" Kaleb asked, wiping at her makeup. He wanted so badly for her to go back being his innocent baby sister.

"Mom—"

"I know. I know."

Kirby held onto her brother for dear life. Seeing Kaleb was surreal. She didn't expect him to be released anytime soon. Him being there was a Godsend because she needed him more than he could imagine.

"I missed you so much," she cried.

"I missed you too."

All of a sudden, Castle walked up behind her. He didn't look happy about seeing Kirby embracing some guy. "The fuck is this nigga?" he asked in a confrontational manner.

Kirby quickly wiped her tears away and turned around. "Castle, this is my brother, Kaleb. He just got out yesterday."

Kaleb stared daggers at the older man. He didn't like the nigga, and that much was evident from his expression. Normal people would've shook hands, but the two men simply mean-mugged each other. Kirby stood in the middle, waiting for one to greet the other first. There was enough tension in the air to slice a knife through.

"Fuck is he doing *here*?" Castle asked. He didn't care how rudely he came off. If Kaleb was expecting a welcome home party then he had another thing coming. It was obvious that Castle didn't appreciate his uninvited presence.

"I came for my sister. Plain and simple. Kirby go pack ya shit," he instructed.

She looked confused for a second, but started to walk off. Castle quickly grabbed her arm, stopping her in her tracks. "Nah. She ain't goin' nowhere, fam."

Kaleb wasn't shaken up in the slightest. He'd faced more intimidating mothafuckas behind bars and he dropped them on their asses without hesitation. He was a little nigga in size, but he had the temperament of a ferocious animal. Castle had definitely met his match.

"The hell she ain't, bruh," Kaleb challenged.

Castle stepped up in the young boy's face. Out of respect, he didn't flat out hit the 19-year old. "Where yo' ass was at, nigga? I been takin' care of *yo'* mufuckin' family while you been locked down playin' tickle booty. Now you think you gon' stroll in this bitch and take what's mine?"

"*What's yours?*" he repeated. Kaleb didn't like Castle referring to his sister like she was his property. "Yo, my nigga, you need to fall back—"

"Or what, young nigga?" Castle snatched his gun out and Kirby's legs almost gave out. He'd snorted a few lines before dinner so he was revved up and ready for combat.

"Kaleb, just go," she said, fearing for his life. Kirby didn't want to see him hurt. She wouldn't be able to live with herself.

"Kirby—"

"Please, Kaleb," she begged. "Just go."

Kaleb looked from her to Castle. He could see the older man had his sister shook, but he wasn't scared of the nigga. As a matter of fact, he had something in store for that ass. Instead of making a scene, he decided to retain his composure and play his hand accordingly.

"Aight...I'mma leave." Kaleb looked specifically at Castle. "But best believe you gon' see a nigga again."

27

"Why did you do that shit?" Kirby rounded on Castle. "That's my brother!"

"Man, fuck that dude." He waved her off. "That mufucka ain't no real nigga. He had ya'll out here fucked up before I came through—"

"He took care of us and he did the best he could!"

"The nigga obviously ain't do enough. Look around! Look how I got you living. Look what I got you pushing now. I'm yo' daddy, yo' brother, and yo' family."

"You sound ridiculous, Castle. And to be honest, it takes a lot to deal with you. I don't need that stress right now. My mother just died. Maybe Kaleb is right. Maybe I should leave with him—"

"And I will kill every mufuckin' thing you *think* you love," he threatened. "Don't ever come at me on that bullshit."

Kirby didn't expect the harsh threat that came from his lips. Castle may've been being a bit too hard, but he couldn't let her young ass go. The only way out of their relationship was in a casket. She knew too much.

Suddenly, Kirby didn't feel so militant.

"I know what it is. You irritable 'cuz you been waitin' for a nigga to drop this dick off in you," he kissed the side of her neck, but she didn't look interested. "Fuck the dinner. Lemme eat you and stroke it."

Kirby tried to push him off. "I'm not in the mood, Castle. My mother just died."

"I'll get you in the mood..."

Before Kirby could dispute him, he picked her up, put her over his shoulder, and carried her to the bedroom. Castle tossed her on the mattress and aggressively removed her clothes before stripping naked.

He was fucked up on coke and Absolut so he didn't notice that she'd already been taken when he shoved it in.

"*Unnnnnhhhh!*" Kirby yelped in pain when he jammed his 11-inches deep inside her. He wasn't even patient or gentle with his penetration. "Castle, it hurts," she complained.

"Shut the fuck up and just relax. Lemme do my thing. It's gon' feel good real soon."

Unfortunately, it never did. Castle pumped ferociously with no regard to her comfort level. He tore her open and didn't stop when he noticed she was bleeding. He assumed he'd popped her cherry, but that was not the case.

"I should've been put this dick in yo' stomach," he groaned. "That's why yo' ass been actin' out. You been waitin' for daddy to fuck you, haven't you?"

Kirby closed her eyes and prayed the torture would hurry up and end.

"Open yo' mouth," he demanded.

Kirby hesitantly did as she was told and he spat in her mouth. "Suck it for me 'til I nut. Get it real wet. Do it just like I taught you."

"Castle, I'm in pain," she complained.

He breathed a sigh of frustration before turning her over. "Fuck it then."

Kirby winced when he entered her from the back.

"Stop running, bay." Castle had to hold her waist just to keep her in place since she kept squirming. After several more painfully deep thrusts, he finally pulled out, and skeeted on her bare ass. "Oh, shit," he shivered. The pussy was like heroin. Panting heavily, Castle collapsed beside Kirby and kissed her shoulder. Semen continued to ooze from the tip of his dick. "Can you clean me up, baby?"

Kirby was disgusted with him. It took everything in her not to slap him. Biting her tongue, she did as she was told with a faltering attitude. Castle slapped her butt when she walked away carrying his cum-filled washcloth.

Kirby tossed it in the bathroom sink and glanced at her reflection. She hardly wanted to look at herself. She always thought she would enjoy her first time with Castle but he made her feel lower than low.

At that moment, the weight of her troubles came down on her shoulders and she cried silently. After taking several moments for herself, she emerged from the bathroom and found Castle snoring loudly in bed.

Tiptoeing past him, she headed to the safe in the den where he stashed cash and drugs. Kirby knew the combination code by heart since she'd saw him open it many times. Turning the dial accordingly, she popped it open, and gazed temptingly at the Ziploc filled with coke.

Without a second thought, she grabbed it...

***

One Week Later

Kirby parked her Benz crookedly in the parking lot of Grip's loft and climbed out. She told him that they needed to talk, but he was just happy to see her again. He'd respectively kept his distance to give her time to mourn.

Grip had no idea that in the midst of doing so she'd rekindled with his uncle.

When Kirby reached his door she knocked loudly. Seconds later, he opened it wearing a wife beater and basketball shorts. His dreads were tied back with a few unruly ones hanging. Grip looked good...but she couldn't focus on that right now.

"Why you knockin'? Where ya key at?" he asked. Grip stepped to the side and allowed her entrance.

Kirby wore a pair of oversized sunglasses, and a white maxi dress with a jean jacket. She sniffled and wiped her nose before crossing her arms. "Lost it," she simply said.

As her drug intake increased so did her irresponsibility. Grip immediately noticed the white residue near her nostrils. She had done a line on her way over while sitting at a red light. Along with her newfound irresponsibility, Kirby had also become reckless. She was spiraling, and she didn't even know it.

"You using now?" he asked, his tone laced with anger. Grip couldn't fathom the thought of her abusing the very shit he peddled.

Kirby quickly said, "No," but her hand automatically went to wipe away at her nose.

"Wassup, Kirby? I been callin' and leavin' you voicemails but you never hit back. I don't be knowin' if you with him or if you just want your space. But I have missed you. How've you been holding up?"

"I'm making it," she said. "But I came to talk to you about something else."

"Wus good?"

Kirby didn't beat around the bush. "We can't fuck with each other, Grip. I want to try and make it work with Castle..."

Grip laughed. "You're fuckin' joking right?"

"Come on now, Grip. Don't act like we both didn't get what we wanted—"

"What? Some pussy?" He looked offended. "You think that's all I wanted?"

"Me and you...we can't do what we've been doing anymore. It ain't right, Grip. I love Castle—"

"You don't love that nigga. You love what he can do for you."

"Don't make this harder than it has to be, Grip."

"If you ain't want a real nigga, what'd you fuck with me for?"

"It was a mistake," she said, staring at her feet.

"Look me in the eyes and tell me that shit."

Kirby met his gaze, but couldn't bring herself to say it. "I—I have to go," she said, turning to leave.

Grip followed her outside. She tried to leave without a full-blown confrontation, but he couldn't let it go so easily. Not when his feelings were already invested.

"Are you fuckin' serious right now?" Grip grabbed her arm and turned her around to face him. "I don't even believe I'm hearin' you right now."

"What'chu want from me, Grip? I love him," she cried. It wasn't because she was upset that caused her tears. It was because she hated the pain she saw on Grip's face. She was telling him one thing, but her heart was screaming another.

"And I love you," he finally admitted.

Kirby tried to pull away, but he wouldn't let her go. "No you don't," she sniveled.

"I love yo' mufuckin' ass. I do," he stressed.

Kirby put up a weak struggle, since secretly she wanted to be held. "No, you don't. Stop saying that."

Grip pulled her closer. "I do. And I know you feel the same."

"I don't." She did. It hurt her to have to lie, but in the end she wanted to protect them both.

"I don't believe that. You just torn right now," he told her.

"And I chose Castle. I'll always choose Castle."

Her words instantly made him release his hold. The comment hit him beneath the belt. Kirby was killing him.

"I'm sorry, Grip."

Kirby turned and rushed to her car where she hopped in and started the engine. The sooner she got away from him the better. She would never forgive herself for what she did, but she knew it was ultimately for the best.

28

Kaleb had just walked out of the *Texaco* gas station when he noticed a pretty face standing at the pump next to his. Shorty was bad as hell. She was a thick redbone with slanted eyes and pouty lips. Her dark brown hair was cut in a Chinese bob. The high-waist jeans she wore hugged her hips and fat ass.

Kaleb definitely appreciated what he saw. If it wasn't for him being there for his sister, he could surely get used to the A. Beautiful women seemingly came in abundance.

When she looked up and noticed him staring she smiled. Apparently, she liked what she saw as well. Kaleb was sexy in loose-fitting pants, a graphic tee, and Nikes. He wasn't with all that skinny-jean wearing shit. He had a simple swag, but the ladies loved it.

"You too damn cute to be pumpin' ya own gas," he told her.

She smiled bashfully.

"Lemme get that for you," he said, walking over. Kaleb took the nozzle from her and resumed pumping gasoline into her Lexus ES. "Who's the handsome lil' guy?" he asked, peering in her backseat. The infant was strapped to his car seat and fast asleep.

"My son," she said, flattered.

"That's wassup. I love kids," he told her. "What's ya name? I ain't gon' be in town long but I'd love to link up. We could grab a bite to eat or somethin'."

"I'd like that," she smiled. "And my name is Luna."

***

A week later, Castle was going through the safe in Kirby's crib when he noticed a shortage in his money and drugs—a few grams to be exact. "I know this bitch ain't been in my shit," he muttered.

Closing the door, Castle headed to Kirby's bedroom. She lay stretched out in the king-sized bed, entangled in its sheets. He took one look at her and knew she was out of it. She was so used to getting blown up in the morning, that she made herself drowsy by afternoon. Kirby had turned into a full on addict right under Castle's nose.

Making his way over to her bed, he smacked her upside the head a few times. "Aye, wake the fuck up!"

Kirby snorted, wiped her nose, and turned on her side. She didn't once open her eyes.

Castle slapped her the second time harder. Kirby woke up instantly then.

"You been in my shit, lil' girl?" he asked, holding up the Ziploc.

Kirby squinted at the drugs in his hands. "No…"

That made him go upside her head again because he knew she was lying. "Bitch, what'chu think? I'm fuckin' stupid? I should make you sell that pussy hole to earn back what the fuck you snorted!" Castle went to the safe and collected the money too. "Bitch, if I can't trust yo' ass then I have no fuckin' use for you."

Kirby staggered out of the bed and went after him. "What are you doing? You don't have to take it—"

"Get the fuck away from me!" Castle pushed her high ass on the floor. "Look at yaself! You a fuckin' disgrace. Get'cho shit together."

Castle stepped over Kirby and headed to the front door. She was more upset that he'd taken the drugs than she was about him leaving.

Fuck him.

Kirby had no problem getting the drugs on her own. Standing to her feet, she grabbed her purse, phone, car keys and left.

"I'm tired of that mothafucka trying to control me while he does whatever the fuck he wants."

Kirby took the elevator to the parking garage. When she reached her car, she unlocked the doors and tossed her purse and keys on the passenger seat. She was just about to climb in when Kaleb stopped her.

"Kirby," he called out. Kaleb slowly approached his sister. He'd been watching her, Castle, and his clique faithfully since he arrived. It was imperative to learn their moves. Ironically, it was pure coincidence bumping into Castle's baby mama earlier. At the time, he didn't know that's who she was.

Kirby didn't look elated about seeing her brother. Unless he could point her in the direction of an 8-ball she had nothing to say to his ass. Her dispassionate greeting was the exact opposite from when she first saw him.

"What do you want? Why are you here? What? You think I'm gonna pack up my shit and leave with you? Fuck you, Kaleb! Everything is your fucking fault! If you hadn't gotten your stupid ass locked up none of this shit would be happening!"

Kaleb allowed Kirby to take her frustrations out on him. She needed someone to blame. "What's happening, sis? Talk to me."

There was sympathy and compassion in his hazel eyes, but all Kirby felt was resentment.

"Just get the fuck away from me, Kaleb," she said, climbing in her car.

In silence, he watched her pull off in haste. Kaleb knew if he didn't act fast he'd lose his sister forever. She was rapidly going downhill. He couldn't lose her too.

Kirby drove downtown and happened upon a day party on Crescent Avenue. The crowd was predominantly white, and it wasn't hard at all to find a plug. By 7 p.m. Kirby was too drunk and high to operate. Her mother's death was taking its toll. She was losing herself, pushing every close person in her life away. Depression left her feeling like she couldn't deal with reality sober. Kirby was killing herself.

Luckily, a patron was nice enough to dial the last incoming call in her log so someone could pick her up. Fortunately for Kirby, that person was Grip.

He came immediately, and collected Kirby from a tattered leather couch in VIP. She was halfway conscious when he carried her out to his truck. "Grip," she slurred. Kirby's head swiveled drunkenly on her neck. She could barely see straight. It was by the grace of God no one took advantage of her.

"I got'chu," he said.

Grip carefully placed her in the passenger seat and secured her seatbelt. He felt partially responsible for her downfall. He knew she needed comfort and moral support, but he chose to stay away because he was bitter about their last encounter. He would never make the mistake of turning his back on her again.

Grip hopped in the driver's seat and started his truck.

"My brother...my brother..." she struggled to say. She was trying to tell him that Kaleb was out, but she was too fucked up to make sense.

"*Ssh*. Just relax and get some rest. I got'chu. I swear I'll never let shit happen to you."

That was the last thing Kirby heard before blackness engulfed her.

***

When Kirby finally came to, Grip was bathing her in a semi-cold bath. Her bra and panties were still on. He was trying to help her come down from her high.

"How'd I get here?" she asked, touching her head. She had a mild hangover. It wasn't even 9 yet.

"You went out and got trashed before the sun even went down. Someone called me and asked if I could come and get you. Now you're here."

Kirby drew her knees to her chest and cried. "Grip...I don't know what the fuck's wrong with me lately. I just feel...lost."

He cupped her chin and turned her head towards him. "Look at me. I'm here for you. Man, you don't have to do this shit to yaself, Kirby. Don't push me the fuck away. I hate to see you going through this shit. Let me be there for you."

Kirby gently grabbed his face and pulled him close. "I'm sorry." She cried and kissed him at the same time. "I'm so sorry, Grip. I love you. I always have."

Grip didn't know if she was saying it because she was vulnerable or if she meant it sincerely. Either way her words touched his heart. He'd never felt as deeply for a woman as he felt for her. "I know. *Ssh.* I got'chu. We gon' be aight," he promised.

"How?" she asked.

"First, I wanna get you the fuck away from that nigga. He fam and all, but he ain't gon' do shit but make it worse."

"Where am I gonna go?"

"I got peoples up in Gladwyne, Pennsylvania. We can lay low there a while. Ya brother's welcome to crash too." Grip assumed he was getting out soon. He had no idea that Kaleb was already out and had visited Kirby.

She'd gotten so wasted that she completely forgot about their conversation earlier. Kirby figured once she was back in PA she could reach out to him. Right now she had no way of getting in touch with him since he didn't leave a number.

"Okay," Kirby agreed. "I'm with it. When will we leave?"

"Tomorrow. But I'll get the ticket's tonight."

"Alright..."

"Trust me, bay. I'm gonna take care of everything."

***

Kirby had Castle so worked up that she pushed him right back in Femi's arms. He thought he was going to go home and be greeted with a hot meal and some pussy, but that wasn't the case.

Castle didn't anticipate on stepping inside an empty house. Femi and Princess were nowhere to be found.

Fuck it. I'll just wait for 'em to get back. I know they miss a nigga, he told himself.

Castle went in the bedroom and started removing his jewelry. After placing his Rolex on the nightstand, he removed his earrings next. The clear back to one of them accidentally dropped on the plush carpet.

Castle leaned down to grab it, but noticed something wedged between the bedframe and nightstand. "The fuck?" Reaching between the surfaces, he grabbed the Breitling and examined it. Castle recognized the watch immediately, because he'd brought it for Aviance on his 20th birthday.

Femi didn't realize the watch had fallen and gotten stuck when she and Castle last fucked. What the hell was his watch doing in their bedroom though?

Castle's stomach dropped to the pit of his stomach when the realization finally slapped him in the face. He squeezed the watch so tightly in anger that the glass face shattered.

Castle rushed to his phone and called Femi up. She didn't answer the first two times, but she finally picked up on the third. "What, Castle? I'm busy—"

"Where the fuck you at?" he pressed.

"I'm doing something. Why?"

Hearing her say that made his blood boil. Had his precious wife really been smashing his homeboy behind his back? "We need to have this mufuckin' conversation in person," he said. "I'm on my way over there. Where you at? Text me the address."

Femi hesitated. "Me and Princess are out looking at houses," she finally admitted.

Castle thought he'd misheard her. "Fuck you lookin' at cribs for?"

Femi paused. She took a deep breath before saying, "Because I want a divorce…"

Castle felt like his entire world had come crashing down. He always expected her to be there to take his shit. But hearing those words tumble out her mouth was a painful reminder that nothing lasted forever. Femi had finally gotten fed up with his shit.

"You tell me this bullshit over the phone? Man, where the fuck you at? Send me the address. Don't make me come looking for you."

Femi reluctantly rattled off the address to where she was. Castle wasted no time as he hopped in his Maserati and raced to Johns Creek, Georgia. He couldn't wait to catch up with Aviance. *I'mma hang that mufucka!*

Castle made it to the home Femi and Princess were at in twenty minutes tops. He had cut off every driver on the road that was in his way. He couldn't get there fast enough.

On the phone, Femi said they were looking at houses, but he didn't see a second car parked in the driveway. Where the fuck was the realtor? His wife didn't want to admit that she'd already closed the deal on the foreclosed home. She was only there to show the place to Princess.

Castle stormed inside the spacious house, yelling Femi's name. He found her standing alone in an empty bedroom with half-painted walls. She looked nervous; guilty.

The moment they made eye contact, Castle held up the watch. Femi almost pissed herself. Her expression said it all.

"YOU BEEN FUCKIN' THIS NIGGA BEHIND MY BACK?!" His thunderous voice bounced off the thin walls.

Femi instantly broke down crying. "Castle, I'm sorry..."

"Bitch, I oughta make you swallow this fuckin' watch!"

"You were always in the streets! You were always cheating on me!"

A deep, guttural scream broke free from Castle's chest. Enraged, he hauled the watch at a nearby wall, denting the surface. His fist connected with it next.

Femi jumped in alarm. She never thought the day would come when Castle discovered the truth. Up until recently, she'd always been so careful.

"Bitch, how could you do that shit?!" he yelled. "Who the fuck are you?!"

"Castle, I'm sorry!" Femi cried. She was afraid that he might whup her ass, but he decided to reveal his own dirt.

"You dumb bitch," he spat. "I fucked Monica three years ago during my Yacht party. Yo' drunk ass was passed out in the next room."

The bomb he dropped made her knees weak. Femi would've preferred him slapping her. "What did you fucking say?" Tears slid off her chin and plummeted to her feet. She didn't want to believe what he just revealed.

"Yeah, swallow that shit, bitch."

"You dirty mothafucka!" she screamed.

Castle laughed wickedly. He enjoyed seeing her pain. He wanted to make her backstabbing ass fold. "Got any other fuckin' secrets you wanna throw out since we admittin' shit?"

Femi laid her cards on the table when she said, "Princess is not your daughter."

Castle's mouth fell open; his heart lurched. It felt like she'd taken a spear and impaled him. He didn't think it was possible to hear something worse than her fucking Aviance.

"BITCH, WHAT THE FUCK YOU JUST SAY?!"

Femi jumped at the sound of his booming voice. She regretted saying it the minute it fell from her lips. Femi chastised herself mentally, but it was too late to take it back. The overwhelming damage was already done.

"Castle, I—"

"Who's is she then if she ain't mine?" he demanded to know.

Femi sobbed hysterically. "Please don't make me say it, Castle—"

"Answer the fuckin' question!" he shouted.

"Benny's!"

Castle staggered backwards like he'd been assaulted. He had to grab the wall just to keep from falling. He'd killed that mothafucka years ago, and the nigga was still winning. Benedict was taunting Castle in the worst way imaginable.

Femi was fucking his brother behind his back? Of all the secrets she had dropped, Castle didn't know which one was worst.

"Princess is almost eighteen... You mean to tell me that lil' girl ain't mine? That lil' girl I raised? That lil' girl that calls me daddy?" Castle's voice cracked as he spoke. Tears filled his eyes before spilling over his lower lids.

Femi had never seen him cry a day in her life. She had broken him and there was no taking it back.

"Was Knight mine?" Castle asked, broken-hearted. "Was that my son?"

Femi didn't answer. She couldn't stop crying. Truthfully, she didn't know. She and Benny had been fucking around well before she first got pregnant.

"*GGGGGGGRRRRRRRR!*" Castle released a sorrowful cry. His entire existence felt like a lie. Femi had robbed him of one of the greatest milestones in his life.

"Castle, I'm so sorry! I made a mistake back then. I love you! You know I love you! That's why I helped you set him up. I've always loved you more."

Castle wasn't trying to hear that shit as he punched the wall repeatedly. When he finally stopped his knuckles were raw and bloodied. Unable to stand the sight of Femi, he left the room in a violent tirade.

Less than two minutes later, Castle burst inside the room again with his gun aimed.

POP!

29

Femi fell against the wall after taking a bullet to the chest. She never saw it coming, and Castle didn't think twice about pulling the trigger. He was so angry that all he wanted to do was hurt her. He didn't regret what he did until he saw her fall to the floor.

Princess sprinted to her mother's aid. She was outside admiring the garden when she heard the gunshot. She had no clue about the chaos occurring indoors.

"Oh my God! What'd you do?" Her voice shook with terror as she tended to her dying mother. "WHAT THE FUCK DID YOU DO?!"

Castle looked from his daughter to Femi lying outstretched with a hole in her chest. He couldn't believe he'd actually shot her. "Femi..." He rushed over to try and console her, but Princess pushed him away. "Get the fuck away from her!" she screamed. "Don't you touch her! You a fucking monster!"

Castle stood there, mouth agape for several seconds. When panic finally settled in, he fled the scene of the crime and headed to his warehouse to regroup.

Meanwhile inside, Femi coughed and choked on her own blood. Her dress shirt was soaked in her DNA. She never expected her day to end like this. "I...have to...tell you...something," she struggled to say.

"Save your energy. I'm gonna call 911. You'll be okay, ma," Princess cried. She regretted ever speaking disrespectful or mistreating her mother. If she knew their time together would be so short she would've been a better daughter. "You're gonna be okay, ma. You're gonna make it." Princess went to retrieve her phone, but Femi stopped her. "Wait...I...need to...tell you this."

Princess leaned her ear close to Femi's bloody mouth and listened.

***

Grip was driving through Smyrna when his cellphone rang. He'd just come from dropping Kirby off at Marissa's apartment. As unusual as that was, it was the only place Castle wouldn't look for her immediately. Grip had just enough time to take care of a few loose ends before flying out in the A.M.

He was on his way to Aviance's crib when he grabbed his phone and looked at the caller ID. It was Princess.

Grip answered the phone and she started going a mile a minute. She was crying and talking so rapidly that he barely could make out a word she was saying.

"P, hol' up. Slow down. I can't hear you."

Princess forced herself to take a deep breath. She then went on to tell him that Femi was currently on the operating table.

"He shot her, Grip! That mothafucka shot her!"

Grip's hands tightened on the steering wheel. Tears blurred his vision as he listened to her explain how Castle set up and killed his father.

***

Grip called all around to everyone to see if they knew where Castle was. Unfortunately, no one had heard from or seen him. It was sunset when he finally went on a whim and visited the warehouse. Surprisingly, he found Castle's car parked out front, and from the looks of shit he was alone.

Grip grabbed his iron before hopping out his truck. Castle was on a rampage, and he knew he couldn't trust him.

Castle was back in the makeshift office, sniffing enough cocaine to OD. The police were already out looking for him, and it'd only be a matter of time before they reigned down on his entire empire. Things couldn't have been anymore fucked up.

Castle jumped and reached for his gun after hearing someone walk in.

"I wouldn't do that shit," Grip said, aiming his piece. He was much faster on the draw. Ironically, Castle had taught him well.

His uncle stared at him with bloodshot, red-rimmed eyes. His mission right now was to get high enough to numb the pain. His phone hadn't stopped blowing up, but he wouldn't dare answer the mufucka. Word traveled fast about what he'd done. The streets were more informative than the news.

Castle held his hands up in mock surrender before slowly standing from the desk. There was a sinister grin on his face. He might've been happier to see police than Grip aiming a pistol at his head. "Why the fuck you here?"

"Why the fuck you think?" Grip shot back. "You thought I was never gon' find out?"

"Hell you talkin' 'bout? Shouldn't yo' ass be somewhere chasin' after my bitch?"

"Been there, done that, bruh. It finally paid off too," he taunted. "You'll never see her ass again either. You can believe that shit."

Castle laughed at his boldness. "You so fuckin' weak. I told yo' ass these hoes ain't shit but setbacks. Pussy nigga, just like Benny—"

He barely finished his sentence before Grip charged and attacked him. Shooting Castle seemed too easy. He wanted to make the arrogant, self-centered bitch suffer.

Grip didn't hold back when he delivered punch after devastating punch. His fists connected with every body part he could reach. Castle dropped after the third blow and Grip resorted to kicking and stomping his chest and head. Grip almost knocked him unconscious after his sole connected with Castle's skull. The back of his head bounced off the cement ground, causing his brain to rattle. His nose immediately started bleeding, and he saw double.

Grip finally stopped after tiring himself out. The ass-whupping had been a long time coming. His chest heaved up and down; sweat glistened on his forehead. He'd beaten the shit out of Castle. He didn't even realize he'd dropped his gun until he noticed it lying next to him.

Grip knelt down and picked it up. His uncle was a bloody, battered mess. In a few short minutes, when the swelling took over, he'd hardly be recognizable.

"Is it true?" Grip yelled. "Did you kill my fuckin' father?" There was so much rage and animosity in his heart. He replayed over in his head everything Princess had told him.

Castle surprised Grip when he started cackling. Not even a beat down could hinder his machismo.

"Answer me, mufucka!" Grip cocked the loaded gun and aimed at Castle's body. He hadn't even tried to get up off the floor. He figured he was a dead man anyway.

"You dumb mufucka..." Castle wiped his mouth and spat blood and a tooth on the ground next to him. "Benny ain't yo' fuckin' daddy, nigga! I am!"

30

Grip was unmoved by the truth. He could've snapped, but somewhere in the back of his mind, he always knew it. Sadly, the revelation wasn't enough to change his sentiments. Grip had no sympathy when he squeezed the trigger.

POP!

A single bullet tore through Castle's torso. His eyes shot open and his face contorted in agony. He didn't think Grip had it in him to shoot him, but apparently he'd underestimated the 20-year old.

Satisfied with his choice, Grip left the room and his father to die alone. It was the same place Anderson was killed. Castle lived by the gun and now he would die by it.

Grabbing his chest, he attempted to call out to Grip. But the only thing that came out was a thick portion of dark red blood. He was bleeding out incredibly fast.

As Castle lay in solitude on the hard concrete floor he couldn't help but reflect on all the people in his life. The niggas in the mafia, the bitches he put up in houses, the so-called friends. He never pictured himself going out alone with no one near to hold his hand. That was the one thing in life he feared. Castle would die alone, a cold, callous man.

***

Grip headed straight to Castle's mansion after leaving him helpless in the warehouse. He planned on dumping that mothafucka's safe and taking off with Kirby a.s.a.p. After today, neither of them would look back.

Grip parked his truck in front of the large Virginia Highlands home and hopped out. Castle's half-witted ass still kept a spare in a fake rock near the front door. After letting himself in, Grip rushed to the huge painting on the wall in the sitting room. Behind it was a 2x2 built in safe.

Castle was so fucking predictable. Grip couldn't believe the nigga actually used his birth year for the combination code. When he opened it, he saw nothing but stacks of money, cocaine, and a variety of pills.

Grip ran through the house and located a duffel bag in the hallway closet. He then proceeded to take the only thing he had use for. Grip didn't take all of it—just enough to survive on for a while. With all the grief Castle caused, he felt like he deserved the shit.

Outside of the house, Kaleb brought Jasmine's BMW to a slow stop. He was strapped and ready to confront Castle. If the nigga wasn't trying to hear him, he had no problem laying his ass down. What Kaleb didn't know was that Grip had already beaten him to it.

Killing the engine, he hopped out and grabbed his nine. He'd just closed the door when Grip bolted out carrying the duffel bag of money.

Kaleb immediately aimed his piece at the giant dread head. He'd seen Grip a couple times while trailing Castle and his crew, but he didn't know he was Kirby's friend.

"Who the fuck is you?" Grip grilled.

"Where that nigga Castle at?" Kaleb asked.

"Who the fuck wanna know?" The sight of the gun-toting pretty boy didn't frighten Grip. If Kaleb squeezed then he would have to kill him, because if he didn't Grip would slaughter him with his bare hands.

"I need you to deliver that nigga a message for me," Kaleb said.

Grip was pissed that he was being held up with such bullshit. Whatever Castle had going on didn't have a thing to do with him. Grip didn't know he was standing toe to toe with Kirby's brother. He quickly lost his temper and dropped the duffel bag. "How 'bout I just beat'cho ass." Grip walked up on him and Kaleb squeezed.

POP!

A single shot to the abdomen stopped Grip in his tracks...

31

Kirby released a deep sigh as she stared at the time displayed on her phone's screen. She hadn't seen or talked to Grip since he dropped her off yesterday. It was twenty minutes until boarding and he still hadn't shown up. If he didn't walk through the doors of the airport soon, they'd miss their flight.

"Where is he?"

Kirby called him for the tenth time but his line went straight to voicemail. It never crossed her mind that something was wrong and his phone was dead. She figured he might've just lost track of time. Sadly, she wouldn't have been able to handle the truth.

For the first time ever, Kirby finally had enough strength to walk away. From the money, from the condo, the clothes, the shoes, the car—from it all. All she wanted was to start over with him.

Kirby took a seat on a nearby bench and patiently waited for the moment when Grip arrived.

***

Princess and her boyfriend Tony quietly made their way inside the dreary warehouse. She was still wearing the same bloodstained clothes from earlier. After leaving the hospital, she headed there immediately.

Grip had texted her while on his way Castle's house, letting her know where he left the nigga stretched out. Princess knew she had to act fast before authorities swarmed the premises. It'd only be a matter of time before they found out about the warehouse and the illegal drugs stored within.

Princess had to see for herself. She deserved to get a good look at his body before a mortician got a hold of him. She and Tony didn't expect to find Castle coughing and wheezing in a puddle of his own blood. The mothafucka was still alive!

A tear slipped from her eye and rolled down her cheek. But it was for her mother— not him.

"I thought you said the nigga told you he killed him."

Princess sniffled and wiped her tears away. "Fuck it. We'll finish his ass," she said. "Hand me the gun..."

Tony passed Princess Femi's tiny pink pistol. Castle had gotten it for her on Valentine's Day back in '08. Princess had no opposition whatsoever about putting Castle out of his misery. His heartless ass deserved every bit of it.

"We gotta be quick," Tony whispered. He watched from behind with a look of approval. Seeing Castle suffer was orgasmic. He wanted to witness the nigga take his last breath.

Princess aimed the loaded gun at her father. "I always hated your ass," she cried.

Castle looked up in her eyes and knew she wasn't about that life. She was truly Benny's daughter. She couldn't even pull the damn trigger.

Castle continued to cough and gurgle on his own blood. He could feel his life slowly slipping away with each second that passed.

"I can't!" Princess bellowed. She wanted to pull the trigger more than anything she ever wanted in life, but she couldn't bring herself to do it.

"Shit, gimme the mufuckin' gun. I can." Tony quickly took the gun from her and stepped up. He was so excited about the opportunity for vengeance that his dick got hard from the adrenaline.

Payback was indeed a mothafucka.

POP!

32

Aviance was among the first to learn of Castle and Femi's plight. The distraction was just what he needed to finally make his move. The niggas McKenzie flew down from Philly were official. They even had a connect ship weapons so that they could execute each lick without compromise.

Mark and Tex were the shooters she called on. Everyone was frazzled with all that happened so it wasn't hard to catch niggas off guard when they stormed in the trap houses.

All four men collected from each spot while McKenzie patiently waited in the car. She wasn't even the getaway driver. She was only there to spectate and make sure everything went as planned.

They bodied each worker at every house so no one would come after them. The mob would feel this hit, and they'd be shocked to find out Aviance was the one behind it. He figured it didn't matter since the Feds would be closing in soon. The organization had drawn too much attention and media with all of the bloodshed.

The last trap house was located in Riverdale. After cleaning the place dry, they dumped the last of the work in the trunk. They were hot as fuck, riding around with over $8 million in coke. They would've hit the warehouse too, but the cops had already swarmed the place. All the kilos inside would be confiscated.

Aviance felt like the man when he hopped in the backseat and snatched off his ski mask. He was the only nigga wearing one since his cowardly ass didn't want his former co-workers seeing his face.

Mark, a chubby dark-skinned dude with shoulder length dreads, hopped on the Interstate. The further he drove away from Atlanta the sooner he would be able to breathe easy. They'd hit six different stash houses in less than two hours. There wouldn't be any evidence left for the police to scrape up when they finally did arrive.

"Now what?" Aviance asked excitedly. He couldn't wait to flip the product and make a fortune.

POP!

All of his plans were halted when Tex shot him in the chest without warning. Blood sprayed the window of the backseat and McKenzie's clothing. She knew it was coming sooner or later, but it still caught her off guard.

Aviance looked down at his shirt as if he needed proof that he'd been shot. It wasn't until he looked over at McKenzie that he realized he'd been set up. It was her idea to rob Castle, but it was Kaleb who'd assembled the plan after learning about his operation.

After corresponding through letters the last few weeks of his imprisonment, Kaleb helped shape and formulate the scheme. Her only job was to convince Aviance to agree to it. They wouldn't have known where the stash houses were without his knowledge.

Kaleb's plan was foolproof. If it wasn't for him intervening she would've fucked around and gotten herself killed. Kaleb took leadership in order to have a successful robbery and that was exactly the outcome. It was he who recommended Mark and Tex to help with the robbery. Back in the day, they used to all steal cars together. Kaleb took the rap for them when he was busted so the niggas owed him big time. They were his boys and down to make an easy come up.

McKenzie willingly followed suit because she'd been in love with Kaleb since she was a girl. She had love for Aviance too, but if she had to choose she'd pick Kaleb every time. Aviance was nothing more than a mere sacrifice. She'd used him to get exactly what she wanted.

Aviance reached for his gun with what little strength he had. McKenzie quickly beat him to the punch as she grabbed it in the nick of time. He would've shot her between her pretty green eyes if he'd gotten to it first.

Aviance was determined to stay alive. He wrapped his hands around her neck and squeezed tightly. "Bitch, I'mma kill you."

"The fuck goin' on back there?" Mark asked. He tried to look over his shoulder to see what was happening, and swerved in the process.

McKenzie was just about to shoot him, but he released his hold and fell against the door. He died right there with his head on the window, slumped over. Castle always told him that pussy would be his downfall and he was right.

Mark's reckless driving drew the attention of a parked cruiser on the interstate. They'd just hopped on 20 when a set of flashing blue and red sirens lit up behind them.

McKenzie's worst fear had come to life. There they were riding hot with $8 mil worth of coke in the trunk, a dead body in the backseat, and several unregistered guns.

Mark refused to slow down. She didn't know how shit would play out, but right now fate was definitely not in her favor.

McKenzie pulled out her phone and attempted to call Kaleb but he didn't answer.

"Shit!" She swallowed the bitter taste of karma. It tasted like shit.

TO BE CONTINUED...

EXCERPT FROM "WHEN A RICH THUG WANTS YOU" BY PEBBLES STARR

ONE

Loud rap music thumped through the speakers of Club Indigo on a Friday evening, and the place was jam packed. Raelyn and her girls, Blue and Symba were among the crowd of club-goers as they shuffled to get to the empty seats at the bar. Though the place was filled to capacity, the three women still managed to stand out. Dressed in designer wear from their head to their thousand dollar shoes, you would've thought they were celebrities—or at least the wives of male celebrities.

Twice, Raelyn had been stopped and asked if she was a reality star from one of Atlanta's many hit TV shows. With a curt smile, she shook her head no, loving every minute of the overwhelming attention.

Rarely did Raelyn go out. As a matter of fact, she barely left the three bedroom luxury condo she lived in—thanks to her overprotective fiancée, Marlon Jetson aka Jett. He could put a teenage daughter's father to shame with how controlling he was.

Truthfully, Jett wasn't feeling the

idea of Raelyn stepping out for the night. He hated whenever she went out parlaying with her attention-seeking girlfriends whom he'd warned her about hanging with.

Jett despised the thought of another nigga pushing up on what he considered was rightfully his. He'd taken Raelyn's virginity five years ago on her 17th birthday, and he would be damned if he let another motherfucker even take a whiff of her goods. Raelyn was his. She knew it. He knew it. And every nigga in a 200 mile radius knew it...Well...everyone except for the tall, dark chocolate, hunk checking her out from across the club.

Nicki Minaj's *"No Flex Zone"* poured through the speakers as Caesar, his partner Canyon, and a few of their closest associates held shit down in the VIP section. Although, he wasn't really the party type, Caesar was a firm believer in keeping up appearances.

A colorful array of women from all different races surrounded them, each one looking for a nigga that would change their life. Even with the lovely selection of women in his face, Caesar only seemed to have eyes for one.

Damn, shawty bad.

In the midst of staring at Raelyn, Caesar noticed a trio of women gawking at their section from across the club.

Whenever he and Canyon stepped out on the scene, everyone ate and drank for free. Small time hoodlums turned big time entrepreneurs they had no problem feeding the fam and anyone wanting to be associated. Finances were the least of their concerns.

Spend that shit without a care in the world. Ain't like you can take it with you when you gone. That had been their motto for years.

Using his index finger, Caesar beckoned the three sexy women to join them in VIP. Smiling from ear to ear, they quickly made their way over to the already crowded section. Champagne bottles popped and marijuana clouds filled the air. As usual, their camp had the place on lock.

As Raelyn navigated through the thick crowd of people, her gaze briefly connected with the guy who'd been peeping her swag. A flock of chicks surrounded him, but yet and still he seemed fixated on her.

Raelyn noted his tall, muscular physique, designer wear, and glowing jewelry. He was fine as hell, and judging from the cocky poise he held she was sure he knew it as well. The way his Givenchy tee hugged his broad chest and made his biceps look almost Hulk-like was hypnotic.

Must be a ballplayer or one of these new rappers out here, she thought.

As soon as Raelyn noticed they'd been keeping eye contact for a bit too long, she quickly tore her gaze away. The last thing she wanted was to give a nigga the impression that she wasn't already taken.

"Damn, I can't believe it's this packed in here!" Raelyn shouted over the blaring bass. She looked stunning that evening in a fitted red Chanel dress and Giuseppe sandals. Jett spared no expense when it came to spoiling her. In his mind, luxuries were the invisible leash he kept tied around his girl so she wouldn't roam.

Standing at an even 5"7, Raelyn's smooth, blemish-free skin was the color of honey. Her long, auburn hair was flat-ironed bone straight, and pulled up into a sleek ponytail which showed off her delicate features. Raelyn's high cheekbones, mint-colored eyes, and piercing dimples made her look almost exotic. Breathtaking would have been an understatement if used to describe her.

Anytime Raelyn stepped in a room she commanded attention. There wasn't a nigga around who didn't stop what they were doing to check her out. And every insecure female made sure to check to see if their man was watching.

"Girl, tell me about it. You'd think the owner was giving away free bottles or some shit," Blue joked.

At only twenty-one, Blue Davenport was the youngest of the trio and the most rambunctious at a mere 4'11. Blue's fair skin was the color of French vanilla, and she wore her long wavy hair aqua blue. Fifty percent of her body was covered in tattoos, and the septum piercing she sported made her look fierce.

Once the girls finally made it to the bar, Symba was the first to order. "Let me get a double shot of Hennessey," she said, placing her custom made clutch on the surface.

At twenty-three, Symba was the eldest, and the most calm of the three. However, Raelyn was sure that her unquenchable thirst for liquor contributed to her docile personality. She didn't talk much about her personal life, and her girls were the closest thing she had to family.

Although Symba fronted like she didn't have a care in the world, she drank herself to sleep every night. And when she wasn't tossing back a shot, she was fucking promiscuously as if it were a hobby. Symba was to sex what an addict was to crack; but luckily her girls never judged her though and that's why she loved them.

Symba was a beautiful brown-skinned woman with plump lips and a fat ass that she always used to her advantage.

Although, her many prospects kept her satisfied there wasn't a single man out there who possessed her heart.

Just seconds before Raelyn ordered her usual—Sex on the Beach—her secret admirer and his patnah approached her and her girls. "Hey, Jessica. Do me a favor and start a tab," Tall, Dark, and Handsome said to the bartender. "Anything they order's on me."

Symba and Blue smiled giddily at one another. There was nothing better to them than having complimentary drinks all night.

Raelyn, on the other hand, looked up and met the penetrating gaze of her admirer. He was even sexier up close in person. In fact, she was surprised he was able to break away from his herd of groupies for two minutes.

Damn, he smells so good too, Raelyn thought to herself.

"How you doin'? I'm Caesar," he said, extending his large hand. The diamond Rolex watch on his wrist sparkled beautifully. His attire was so flashy that Raelyn barely even recognized the foreign designer wear. She would be lying to herself if she said his swag wasn't on point.

"And I'm engaged," Raelyn smiled, holding up her ring finger. The $8000 round-cut ring sparkled beautifully. She was always ready to show it off at the drop of a dime, but never quick to admit that the piece of jewelry was in fact stolen.

Grinning slightly, Caesar held his hands up in mock surrender. "Aight then, Miss Lady. My aim isn't to step on anyone's toes. Just wanted to be the fiftieth dude tonight to tell you how beautiful you are."

Raelyn smirked, but held her composure. Compliments came to her naturally. However, something about hearing it from a well-dressed stranger made her blush just a little. "Thank you."

Caesar smiled, revealing a perfect set of pearl white teeth. "Look, if you and ya girls—or you and ya man come through again, drinks on me. I'm the owner," he told her. "It was nice meetin' you, aight. You enjoy yaself."

Raelyn smiled, clearly impressed by chivalry. "You too. And thank you again," she replied sweetly.

"Always," Caesar said before walking off.

On cue, his fine ass brown-skinned friend followed suit—but not before winking at Symba.

With how drop dead gorgeous Caesar was, Raelyn knew he wouldn't have a problem finding the next chick. *Bitches nowadays are like vultures for a nigga with a little paper in his pockets.*

Caesar kept his cool as he swaggered off. He could still feel Raelyn's eyes watching him even though she told him she wasn't interested. Although he didn't get any play, he refused to be a dick just because she had a nigga.

Money wasn't shit to him; neither was getting pussy, and he was far from being careless with either. At twenty-six, Caesar was far more mature than niggas twice his age. A young boss, he looked and conducted himself as such. And one thing was for certain; leaders didn't sweat the small shit—especially women.

Maybe I'll run into her again under different circumstances, Caesar thought.

He'd put a seed in Raelyn's ear, and that was all that mattered at the end of the day. All he had to do was play his hand right the first time.

"Damn, Ray. You cold, bitch," Blue cackled. "That nigga was fine as fuck! And fresher than a new pair of kicks."

"*And* selfless!" Symba added, holding up her complimentary beverage. She loved a nigga that wasn't scared to break bread.

"Duly noted," Raelyn smiled. "But ya'll hoes must've forgotten that I gotta man at home—"

"Bitch, you've been wearing that rock for the past two years," Blue reminded Raelyn.

"Right! My damn bridesmaid's dress is collecting dust in the fucking closet," Symba teased. "You stay squawking about that wedding that ain't even happened yet—"

"It's *gonna* happen," Raelyn stressed.

"When?" Blue hounded. "'Cuz from the looks of shit, it seems like Jett put that rock on you just to prove a point."

Raelyn was now becoming annoyed. "And what point is that? Please enlighten me."

"That you're *his*," Symba chimed in. "So niggas like the nice one you just passed up on don't stand a chance! I'm telling you, Raelyn, that motherfucker just wants to make a statement. I mean, think about it—"

"Look, I'm not trying to *think about it*. And I'm definitely not 'bout to do this with ya'll here," Raelyn waved them off. "I just wanna enjoy myself, okay. Can we do that?" She then lifted her glass, motioning for a toast.

"Hell yeah," Symba smiled. Beef between them never lasted long, and most times it was completely nonexistent. The three friends were tighter than a virgin female.

"Shit, I'll drink to that," Blue sang,

clinking her shot glass against theirs.

NOW AVAILABLE!

EXCERPT FROM "ENAMORED BY HIS CHARM"
BY PEBBLES STARR

1

VERA

"I want you to get the fuck out my house!"

My chest heaved with anger as I yelled at the top of lungs. I was so upset that I barely could breathe, think straight, or formulate the proper dialogue to stress how fucking upset I was. The only words I seemed able to emit were that I wanted him out. Out of my apartment, out of my life, out of my system.

It took everything in me not to haul off and punch Trey. I was at my wits end with him. There were no more chances in me to give him, no more benefit of the doubt left to spare. I was done. *Finito!*

My nostrils flared in anger as I watched his whore dress hastily. I was tempted to pop one of her fake tits. She was pretty, slim, and fair skinned—the complete opposite of myself.

Coming home to find your man in bed with another woman was hell, but the fact that my confidence was now crushed just added insult to injury. Seeing that bitch reminded me of my own insecurities.

I was average with a decent figure and a few extra pounds. I didn't have the big ole' ghetto booty most guys lusted after. Half the time I didn't wear makeup and I wasn't the most fashion savvy woman. I was as normal as normal got.

"Vera, let's just talk about this," Trey said, snapping me from my thoughts.

I didn't even notice him pull on a pair of sweats. I must've been too angry. Just two seconds ago, I'd caught him with his dick out coated in her wetness. The motherfucker didn't even have enough decency to wear a condom.

Tossing my hands up defensively, I said, "There ain't shit to talk about, Trey! I don't wanna hear it! Just get the fuck out!"

Trey took a few steps towards me. He thought I was playing. Without warning, I rushed to the walk-in closet and reached for the top shelf. He must've known what I was retrieving because he started flipping out.

"Hurry up, ma! You gotta get the fuck on!" he told his whore.

She barely made it to the bedroom door before I stormed out of the closet wielding a polished 9mm. My father had been a cop for nineteen years before he was gunned down on my fifteenth birthday. We visited the shooting range religiously. I spent more time there than a kid did playing video games. My aim was impeccable, and Trey knew that shit.

"Man, chill, Vera with that crazy shit! Put the gun down!"

I was pleased with the look of fear in his eyes, but not quite satisfied so I cocked the weapon.

His whore made a daring attempt to run out the room. She was still topless, but determined to put some much-needed space between her and the armed lunatic. I couldn't let her ass off that easily so I took off running after her.

NOW AVAILABLE!

Made in the USA
Lexington, KY
10 October 2016